PRAISE FOR CHRIS STEWART

SHATTERED BONE

"Stewart writes with . . . Clancy's knack for spinning a thrilling global techno yarn."

—CNN Sunday Morning, Off The Shelf

"A top-notch techno-thriller. . . . An impressive debut, complete with suspenseful action, plausible geopolitical scenarios, and authoritative detail."

—*Kirkus Reviews*

"*Shattered Bone* is a splendid thriller."

—W.E.B. Griffin, author of the best-selling series *Brotherhood of War, The Corps,* and *Honor Bound*

"Stewart [ranks] with Coonts and Brown as pilots who can make the reader feel like have joined them in the cockpit for a desperate mission in the enemy skies."

—*Flint Michigan Journal*

"Knuckle-whitening flying scenes. A terrific novel."

—Douglas Preston, best-selling co-author of *The Relic*

"A new technothriller star has been launched. If you enjoy books where the action starts with a bang on the first page and ends with a bang on the last, you'll devour *Shattered Bone.*"

—*Tulsa World*

THE KILL BOX

"A commando-lean plot with nick-of-time saves and edge-of-your-seat theatrics."

—*Publishers Weekly*

"A thriller writer who knows how to deliver."

—*Flint Michigan Journal*

"The plot builds to a page-flipping climax."

—*Booklist*

"I haven't read a novel this interesting and insightful since *The Hunt for Red October*. I commend Major Stewart for his alert mind and creative pen."

—Congressman James V. Hansen, Senior Member, House Armed Services Committee

THE THIRD CONSEQUENCE

" . . . sets Stewart alongside top techno-writers like Clancy and Bond, as his mix of fact and fiction explodes off the page with the immediacy of a live CNN war-zone video feed. Stewart . . . offers up strong characters, a credible plot and a quirky, satisfying finale."

—*Publishers Weekly*

"Pins the reader to the seat of his pants."

—Eric L. Harry, author of *Arc Light*

"Fast and furious. The author writes in a crisp style and tells the story with a certain authentic touch."

—*Stars and Stripes*

THE BROTHERS

THE GREAT AND TERRIBLE

VOLUME 1 – PROLOGUE

THE BROTHERS

CHRIS STEWART

SALT LAKE CITY, UTAH

Other titles by Chris Stewart
(published by Penguin Putnam or St. Martin's Press)

Shattered Bone

The Kill Box

The Third Consequence

The Fourth War

Visit us at DeseretBook.com

Library of Congress Cataloging-in-Publication Data

Stewart, Chris, 1960–
Prologue : The Brothers / Chris Stewart. (The great and terrible, vol. 1)
p. cm.
ISBN 978-1-59038-090-1 (v. 1 : alk. paper)
1. Spiritual warfare—Fiction. 2. Good and evil—Fiction. I. Title.

PS3569.T4593G74 2003
813'.54—dc22 2003021134

Printed in the United States of America
Publishers Printing, Salt Lake City, UT

15 14 13 12 11

For my children.

Witnessing the power and character they bring into this world has convinced me beyond doubt that this generation will rise up "clear as the moon, and fair as the sun, and terrible as an army with banners" (Doctrine and Covenants 5:14).

Acknowledgments

Many people played a critical role in the writing of this book. I can't tell you how many times I sat down with various members of my family to hash out different concepts that can be found on these pages. In addition, there were a few special friends who played an important role. I thank you all for your insight and wisdom.

I also want to thank Sheri Dew and Emily Watts at Deseret Book, for they believed in this project, even on those brief occasions when I had lost faith myself.

Finally, and most importantly, I must thank my wife, Evie. She is my constant beacon, and I am grateful for the spiritual insights she has brought not only to this book but to every aspect of the life we share together.

Author's Note

With the exception of the prologue and afterword, the story in this book takes place in the premortal world. As you will see, I was forced to take author's license in many of the details presented in this book. The simple fact is that we know very little of what life was like for us in the premortal world, and the war in heaven is a mystery we know even less about. Yet any literary work, especially fiction, requires some sense of time, location, conflict, and description in order for readers to allow themselves to be pulled into the story. Without descriptions of human emotions, physical settings, and some sense of timing, the story turns out to be little more than a series of conversations which, although interesting, certainly aren't enough to keep a reader involved.

For these reasons, I was forced to include elements of this mortal life that may not have actually been found in the premortal world. These are included to help provide a setting and an atmosphere for the story. In addition, even though we obviously belonged to one great family there, I have theorized that there might have been some sort of organizational structure that broke us down into smaller groups, which I refer to as "families," and I have referred to members of those smaller groups as "brother" and "sister." If there are details, symbols, or descriptions with which you take issue, I ask for your understanding.

And though my primary goal has been to entertain, it has always been my hope that I might provide a greater sense of our purpose and place in this world. If I have been able to do that, I am very grateful.

And now I show unto you a mystery,
a thing which is had in secret chambers, to bring to pass
even your destruction . . . and ye knew it not.

—DOCTRINE AND COVENANTS 38:13

Ye hear of wars in far countries, and you say that
there will soon be great wars in far countries, but ye
know not the hearts of men in your own land.

—DOCTRINE AND COVENANTS 38:29

Prologue

THURSDAY, APRIL 17
ARLINGTON NATIONAL CEMETERY
WASHINGTON, D.C.

It had rained all night, thunderclouds rolling in from the Blue Ridge Mountains, dark and boiling with power as they met the moisture from the sea. Lightning and heavy rain pounded the night, then suddenly stopped as daylight drew near. The first line of storms moved off to the Chesapeake Bay and lingered over the sea, caught between the rising sun and the musky coastline behind. The rain wasn't over. What was already the wettest spring in a century had much more to give.

The day dawned cold and dreary. Another band of dark clouds gathered in the morning light, moving in from the west, blowing over the hill that lifted on the horizon. Heavy mist hung in the air until the weak morning breeze finally carried it away.

The grass around the freshly dug grave was wet and long, with tiny drops of moisture glistening from the tips of each blade. The pile of dirt next to the grave was dark and rich, loamy with many years of rotting vegetation and now rain-soaked and wet. A green patch of synthetic AstroTurf had been placed over the pile of dirt and pinned down on the corners to keep it from flapping in the wind. A sad arrangement of plastic roses and baby's breath sat atop the fake grass.

The eternal flame at John F. Kennedy's grave site was eight hundred feet to the north, just over the hilltop from the open grave. The Tomb of the Unknowns, Arlington cemetery's most revered site, was hidden behind a crescent of budding oak trees, the lime-green blossoms adding color to the dreary spring morn. Arlington House stood at the crest of the cemetery's highest hill, its white pillars shining against the backdrop of storms. For more than thirty years before the Civil War, Arlington House, with its rolling plantation, slave outbuildings, huge oaks, and cool springs, had been the home and refuge of General Robert E. Lee—until halfway through the war, as a bitter insult to the Confederate general, the northern army had turned his plantation into a cemetery for their dead. Soon after the war, the national cemetery was created, and the transformation was complete. Arlington had become sacred ground.

Few were granted the honor of having their bones put to rest there. But an increasing number were granted the privilege each day.

Too many. Too often.

One of the dark reminders of war.

* * *

The six-man color guard waited by the grave. Their uniforms were so crisp they almost cracked as they moved, their boots so highly polished they reflected the gray light from the sky. Tiny blades of wet grass clung to the sides of their boots and the cuffs of their pants, for the soldiers had walked to the grave from their previous detail, cutting across the enormous cemetery, down the hill next to Arlington House and across McClellan Drive.

The sergeant in charge stood in front of his men, giving

them one final inspection before the mourners appeared. He straightened a shoulder board and tightened a shirt here and there. “Gig line!” he hissed to a young NCO. The junior soldier looked at his chest and aligned the buttons on his shirt with the zipper cover on his pants. “Cover,” the sergeant whispered as he moved down the line. A corporal, a twenty-two-year-old Marine from the Mississippi delta and the youngest member of the team, adjusted his headgear, pulling it down uncomfortably over his eyes. Satisfied, the noncommissioned officer moved to the end of the line, put himself in position, and glanced at his watch. 14:56. The service was scheduled to begin at 15:00 straight up, and, of course, it would begin exactly on time. Precision. Correctness. Attention to detail. That was the way it was done. Perfection was the standard when it came to paying respect to their dead.

The sergeant heard the soft clop of hooves coming up the narrow strip of asphalt that wound through the national cemetery. Glancing to his right, he saw the horse, a single mare, old and slow but still proud, her dark mane perfectly curried and braided to the right. She emerged from around a tight bend in the road, drawing a small carriage behind her. The carriage, black and shiny, with huge wooden wheels and a black leather harness, carried a single bronze casket on its flat and sideless bed. Seeing the casket, the sergeant took a deep breath and straightened himself. *“Ten-HUT!”* he whispered from deep in his chest, the order nearly silent, yet crisp and powerful, and his soldiers drew themselves straight, their shoulders square, their chins tight, their hands forming fists at their sides, their elbows slightly bent into powerful bows. They looked straight ahead, their faces without expression, as they stared at some unknown object on the distant horizon. The sergeant gave a final inspection, barely turning his head, then took another deep breath and lifted his chin. The air smelled of dirt and rain and freshly cut grass. It smelled like the country, reminding him of his home.

As the funeral procession approached, the team leader placed his right foot exactly behind his left, his toe pointing down, barely touching his heel, and turned with precision so perfectly it looked almost mechanical. He faced the approaching wagon, staring at the metal casket so as to never make eye contact with the mourners who followed behind. The dark horse walked with high steps, proudly aware of the role that she played. She held her head tall, her flanks glistening with sweat.

The wagon drew close, and the sergeant felt his heart quicken. This one was special, and he wanted it right.

As the wagon passed under a huge oak tree, he caught a better glimpse of the casket, a dark bronze box draped in an American flag. Atop the flag an enormous ring of flowers, fresh cut and beautifully arranged, had been placed over the center of the casket.

Twenty-four roses. Twelve red and twelve white.

White roses for virtue. Red roses for blood.

Seeing the flowers, the sergeant had to swallow against the catch in his throat. He knew this dead soldier's story—it had been in the papers for the past several days—and though he felt a deep sense of pride in each funeral ceremony he participated in, this one had cut him and he felt unprepared for the emotion inside.

That others might live, he repeated to himself. He swallowed again as he thought of the phrase. It was for only this concept that a fellow soldier had given his life.

The color-guard officer glanced at the carriage again. Next to the roses, glistening in the cool, humid air, a copper medallion and white ribbon had been carefully draped over the stars on the flag. For the first time in his life, the soldier saw the Medal of Honor, the most sacred tribute a nation could bestow on a man. The Medal of Honor was rarely given; ten thousand soldiers might die in battle and not one of them earn the privilege of receiving this award. Indeed, most soldiers would serve their entire careers without meeting a recipient of the Medal of Honor. It was rare, it was sacred, and too often it was given to men who were dead.

The sergeant dropped his eyes to the medal, which glistened on top of the flag. Beside him one of his soldiers sucked in a quick breath. His men stood stone-cold still as the funeral procession approached, the mourners following the carriage as it moved to the grave. And though the sergeant didn't focus on the family, he couldn't help but see her out of the corner of his eye.

She was small, maybe six or seven, with straight, blonde hair, tiny arms, and huge, wondering eyes. She glanced around anxiously, a bewildered look on her face, fear and pain bleeding through the tight look in her eyes. Her mother walked at her side, a perfect reflection of the child: long blonde hair, dark features, and wide, sullen eyes. She was tall and slender and dressed in a simple white dress. No black clothes, the sergeant noticed, no black veil or dark, mournful hat. The woman was young, perhaps only a year or two older than he, and there was something about her, something strong and wonderful. What it was exactly he would never know, but he would always remember the look in her eyes.

Even in their sadness, the mother and daughter were beautiful. They had a look of elegance, with their high cheekbones and light skin, their faces somber but peaceful as they held themselves high. They walked hand in hand, the mother matching the small steps of the girl, both of them misty-eyed but determined somehow. The child approached the grave like it was a terrible monster, a dark, gaping passage leading into the next world.

Thunder broke behind the soldier and rolled through the trees, deep, sad, and somber, the sound echoing across the wet ground as another clap rolled and slowly faded away. A cold breeze blew at his neck, raising the hair on his arms. *Please, Lord,* the soldier prayed. *Hold up your hand. Give this family twenty minutes before you let your rains fall.* Another clap of thunder rolled across the green, rolling hills. It echoed off the grass, which was still glistening and wet. Then came another flash of lightning. But the rains didn't come.

The soldier had performed a hundred ceremonies over the past eleven months; indeed, this was the third funeral ceremony he had presided over today. But as he watched the black wagon and proud horse, as he saw the tiny child holding to her mother's hand and the Medal of Honor over the blue and white flag, he just couldn't hold back the emotion that boiled inside. A single, salty teardrop rolled down his cheek to settle on his jaw before slowly sliding down his neck.

Too many funerals. Too many good men. Too many young children and too many wives.

White roses for virtue. Red roses for blood.

The small family approached, stepping across the wet grass while staring into the darkness of the open grave. The army chaplain, a young major, escorted them as they walked, then reached out and took the mother by the hand to direct her to a white wicker chair. The mother and child sat down carefully, all the while holding hands, the young girl gripping tightly, holding on for dear life. She sat in a small wicker chair, like her mother's, and leaned into her. Her white dress fell to her ankles as she reached down to press the wrinkles from her lap. A tiny crown of white flowers had been braided through the child's hair, and she tugged at them gently to keep them in place.

The mother and child didn't look at each other as the horse-drawn wagon approached and came to a stop. The funeral procession moved forward and formed a half circle on one side of the grave. It was a large group, unusually so, with many more children than one would expect. Two young men, clearly brothers, took up a position behind the young wife. Beside them, the deceased soldier's parents stared solemnly at the casket. The father fought to hold himself together, but the mother seemed more accepting, indeed, she seemed almost at peace. As the family members gathered behind the young wife, the father reached down and placed his hand on the widow's shoulder, and she leaned her face over to rest it on his hand. To the side of the family stood members of the military: enlisted soldiers, young officers, and—to the surprise of the sergeant—a couple of high-ranking generals.

Outside the family ring, and away from the other military members, stood three other military officers, each of them wearing formal dress uniforms, their ribbons and badges displayed on their chests. Two of the officers wore Army green: olive jackets and green pants with a black stripe down the sides. The other officer wore Air Force blues with silver wings on his chest. The three officers were young, all lieutenants, though there was a shadow on their faces that seemed to age them somehow. Between the three lieutenants was a small, dark-haired boy, maybe seven, maybe eight, with olive skin, a hollow face, and gaunt, darting eyes. The sergeant recognized his face from the pictures in the press. He was the only one who had been rescued, the only one who survived. The little boy glanced quickly at the daughter, then down at the dirt. He looked weary, almost guilty, his face clouded with shame. One of the officers noticed his reaction and reached for his hand. He knelt down and whispered, but the child didn't respond.

The chaplain nodded to the color-guard leader, an almost imperceptible movement of his head, and the sergeant commanded under his breath, "Element, post!" The six men moved forward in perfect step toward the carriage, taking up a position with three of them on each side of the casket. Without any verbal commands, the men reached out and took the casket by the metal handles and lifted together. The casket was light, for it was nearly empty; a few pieces and parts were all that remained.

The color guard turned crisply, carried the flag-draped casket forward, and placed it over the nylon straps that had been stretched across the grave. Then they stepped to the side and out of the way. The chaplain walked to the casket and paused, then turned to the family in the white wicker chairs. He leaned over and spoke a few words to the mother, then stood and announced, "Lieutenant Calton's brother has been asked to dedicate the grave."

The color-guard soldier listened carefully. This was something new. Dedicate the grave? He didn't know what that meant. He watched from under the brim of his hat as one of the brothers broke from the crowd, moved to the graveside, and reverently bowed his head.

The prayer was simple and pleading, and tears flowed as the brother spoke. As he concluded his prayer, the young man turned to the casket, took a short step toward it, and placed his hand on the flag. Then he turned to sit down, but he seemed unable to move. He stared at the widow and the fatherless child, then lowered his hand and bowed to one knee as he reached again for the flag. "You were always my hero," he whispered through his tears. "I will love you forever. And I will never forget." He knelt there a moment, his hand touching the flag, then forced himself to stand. The chaplain moved to his side, and the brother stepped back to his place.

The chaplain straightened his uniform quickly, then began to speak. Less formal than most, he spoke slowly and comfortably, but with great authority. It wasn't his intention to preach, he explained, and besides, most of what had to be said, most of the comfort there was to be given, had already been spoken in the service before. But he felt an obligation, as well as a desire, to say some words to the family, if he could.

He spoke of simple things: duty and honor and bravery and truth. He spoke of the obligations that come with freedom and the price that had been paid to keep a people free. Then he nodded to the young widow and lowered his voice. "I cannot help you," he said, speaking directly to her. "In a moment such as this, there is little comfort I can give. Indeed, were I to say too much, my words might only diminish your loss. Only time and the Lord can ease you of this pain. But though I don't have the answers, this much I believe:

"All men will die. All men will be called upon to pass through the veil. But only a few, only a few special men, only those who have been worthy to answer a calling from God, are given the honor to die for a cause.

"And in this life, in these times, all of us will be called on to make a sacrifice. When, or in what manner that sacrifice may be required, only God knows. All we can do is wait and prepare and pray that when our time comes, we will be ready to complete the task that he gives, so that when it is over, when we have done all we could, we might look to the Lord and say the same words he said:

> *'I have fought my way through,*
> *'I have finished the work Thou didst give me to do.'*

"If we can reach that point, if we can say these words to

the Lord, then our sacrifice will be over and he will bring us home."

The chaplain paused as he clasped his hands in front of his chest and looked again at the wife. "I am so proud of your husband," he said in a low voice. "I am so grateful there are still men like him in this world. He fought for the freedom of others. That is the way that we do it here in America. That is the way we fight wars. We don't go looking for battles. We don't conquer other nations; we don't occupy other lands. Indeed, the only foreign soil our nation has ever claimed have been tiny spots such as this, where we seek a quiet pasture to bury our dead.

"And so, Mrs. Calton, I speak for a thankful nation when I tell you that we are not only grateful to your husband, we are also grateful to you. We are grateful for your sacrifice and the price you have paid. Your sacrifice is sufficient. Lieutenant Calton is home. And I pray the Lord will bless you until you are together again."

The chaplain stopped, wiped a hand across his face, then took a step back and nodded to the color guard. Two of the soldiers stepped to the casket and lifted the American flag. Another sergeant marched to the side of a huge tree, a dark oak up the hillside, which would watch over the grave. The sergeant lifted a silver bugle and began to play "Taps."

Day is done
Gone the sun
From the hill, from the dell, from the sea . . .

The sound was low and mournful, and it trailed through the trees and across the wet grass, melting over the graves of the American dead. As the bugler played, the two soldiers reverently folded the American flag into a perfect triangle, tight and tucked in. The junior NCO then held the flag, clutching it with crossed arms at his chest. The team leader took two steps back and briefly stood at rigid attention, then quickly drew his fist from his thigh and up across his chest, extending his fingers as his hand crossed his heart then upward until his finger touched the tip of his brow. He held the salute, the last salute, for a very long time, then slowly, respectfully, almost unwillingly lowered his hand. He stepped forward, took the flag, and, turning crisply, handed it to the young wife. "On behalf of a grateful nation," he said.

She reached out and took it, placing it on her lap. The soldier then passed her the Medal of Honor, and she clutched it in her hand. The two soldiers turned together and moved to the side. The bugle faded away and the silence returned.

And with that it was over. The service was done. At least it should have been over. But none seemed willing to move, for it was almost as if something were yet left unsaid. Every eye turned to the family, those who had lost their husband, father, and son. The young mother glanced down at her daughter, and the child nodded her head. The mother smiled encouragingly, and the little girl stood up. She moved to the casket, which gleamed even in the dim light, then turned hesitantly to her mother, who nodded again. The crowd waited in silence. It seemed even the earth held its breath.

The little girl stood for a moment, and the clouds seemed to part. The wind turned suddenly calm and the thunderclouds paused. The girl placed her hand on the casket and lifted her head. "Daddy, I want to tell you something," she said in a quivering voice. "You are my hero. I want to be just like you. But I don't know if I'm strong enough. I don't know if I can. But I will take care of Mommy, just like you asked me to. I will make her cakes for her birthdays, just like I promised I would. I will be her best friend. I will not leave her alone. And I will try to be strong. But I'm a little bit scared." Her voice trailed off, and she looked quickly away. "I love you, Daddy. I miss you," she said again to the skies. "I need you here, Daddy, and I don't understand. I wish that I could. I want to believe what you said . . . "

She lowered her head in frustration and clasped her arms at her chest, holding herself as if in an embrace. No one spoke, no one moved. Time seemed to stand still, for there was a reverence in the moment that no one was willing to break. How much time passed, it was impossible to say, but the little girl, sweet and peaceful, eventually lifted her head. Her eyes opened and her face seemed to shine.

If she had seen a vision, it was not shared with anyone.

But the heavens *had* been opened.

And she *did* understand.

For they were set to be a light unto
the world, and to be the saviors of men.

—Doctrine and Covenants 103:9

chapter one

THE PREMORTAL WORLD,
IN THE OPENING DAYS OF THE WAR

Michael, the commander, stood at his window, his huge shoulders barely moving as the shudder passed through his chest. His lower jaw trembled, and he clenched down on it. He stared out, alone, as a sadness so deep it penetrated to the core of his soul fell over him like a blanket of blackness and despair. He felt the anger of betrayal and the pain of losing a friend, and worse, the frustration of knowing he'd made a horrible mistake. He looked out on the great city but saw nothing there, his mind completely preoccupied with his own hurt and self-doubt.

How could this happen? How could it go this far? He was his brother—one of his closest friends!

No! He's the enemy, a betrayer, the most dangerous man I know.

He was a fellow warrior.

But he hates you! He'll destroy you! Ambition and power are all he cares about now!

He was a comrade, a great leader in a position of authority. He was loved by the people . . . no, he was more than loved, he was adored. He was an almost mystical figure, with a passion and persuasion that could carry men's hearts.

He was a brother.

He's a traitor. He is the enemy now.

Michael continued to stare out the tall window, then pushed his hands angrily through his hair. His lieutenant stood back, a look of sadness on his face. The commander glanced toward him and saw the concern in his eyes. How many times had this lieutenant pledged his undying support, given an oath to follow him anywhere, to go with him down to the very pit of despair? And yet here Michael stood in his weakness, a weakness he couldn't control. He flushed in frustration. His men shouldn't see him this way.

Yet even now, in his weakness, the commander emanated an uncommon strength, his power and authority bringing light and energy to the room. He was tall and proud, with strong shoulders and powerful arms. His clothes were perfectly tailored and fit neatly over his frame. And though he was young (though not nearly as young as he looked), it didn't take a long observation to determine that the strength of his royalty ran thick in his veins.

It was no trick of fate that Michael found himself in this place, holding this position at this treacherous time. He was born to this duty, his soldiers were certain of that, sired and appointed to lead them in this hour. And to some degree, it was true. From the time he was young, Michael had prepared himself for the battle he would see in his days.

Some called it the last days. Some called it the end. But the truth was, it was both end and beginning. For as one door in life closed, another door opened up, and time had a way of slipping into the next phase.

The commander's shoulders drooped wearily as he stared

out the great window, the afternoon sun pouring over his face.

His quarters, a huge granite structure just outside the main downtown plaza, sat on a small hill surrounded by green lawns and a series of interconnected pools. Various fowl splashed in the water and rested in the tall grass on the banks. The sky was clear and cloudless and blue—so blue it almost seemed painted, like a color that had been selected from a mystical palette. From his window, he could see to the west and north, to the mountains in the distance, and the desert on beyond the great lake.

He stood there a moment, his breathing heavy and slow, then glanced to his lieutenant, one of his most trusted aides. "Jacob," he said slowly, "let me ask you something." A long moment of silence followed. "Can you remember when . . . ?" He stopped, his voice trailing off.

The lieutenant stood in silence, a respectful distance away. Michael glanced at him awkwardly. "How far back can you remember?" he pressed.

The lieutenant shifted his weight. "Sir?" he questioned hesitatingly.

"How far back can you go? What is your earliest memory?"

"I don't know," Jacob answered. "I don't often look back. Today and right now, that's all I think about. We've all worked so hard to get here. It's the only thing that matters to me."

The commander took a deep breath. "He and I grew up together. Did you know that?" he asked.

Jacob nodded. Everyone knew that. It was often mentioned in conversation.

Michael folded his arms behind his back, interlocking his fingers, his shoulders square, his head low. "I remember us walking together in a meadow somewhere," he reminisced.

"It was raining. We were laughing, playing, and soaked to the core. It was a pure moment of joy. I can picture it so clearly still; I can feel it even though it was such a long time ago. Even now, sometimes when I smell the wet grass, I can't help but think of that time. The smell takes me back. It is a wonderful memory.

"From the time I was young, he was always around. We were always together, almost every day. So tell me, Jacob, because I would really like to know. How could two men, close as brothers, set out on the same path, yet come to such different conclusions as to what matters in life?"

Jacob's brow furrowed, and he was slow to reply. "I can understand a few things, but I don't understand that. Why people change, why they choose to hate and betray; I've seen it enough now, but I don't understand why.

"But sir, if I may, there was no way you could have known. Even the Father . . . "

"No, Jacob," the commander cut him off. "I wanted to try to save him, but I was warned that I would fail."

"Sir, perhaps. But you had to try; you had to let it play out. That was the only way you could know. And it would have been unfair to presume until it had proven true."

"Yes, . . . well. But it is clear I was wrong. And now we all know."

The lieutenant nodded slowly. "Yes, sir, we do."

Michael was silent a moment, pondering the seriousness of his mistake. The precious time and effort trying to redeem his friend—how many souls had been lost because of it? How much more serious was the problem now than it might have been if he had acted more quickly to contain it? He took a breath, squared his shoulders, and drew up his strength. "How deep does it go?" he asked somberly.

"Very deep, sir. He is powerful now."

"Tell me."

"The floodgates have opened. Many who we thought would stay on our side have openly pledged their loyalty to him. He has been working in the dark for months, even years, building a strong base of support. He is a master of darkness and secrecy. He has a great following, and he gains more strength every day."

"I need to call the Council together . . . "

"Yes, sir, I agree. Before you do there's something else you need to know."

Michael eyed his lieutenant, a stern look on his face. "What is it?" he demanded.

"Sir, it is difficult for me to be in this position. It really would be better if you were to hear it from—"

"No, Jacob. Now. I want to hear it from you."

The lieutenant shook his head as he lowered his eyes. He spoke in a whisper, for the words were poison to him. "He is drawing up papers to have you removed. He claims you have betrayed us. He says you must be destroyed."

"He accuses *me*?" Michael answered.

"Yes, sir, he does. He claims that you have sought to betray the Father, that you have a secret pact, together with some others, to bring the government down. He says he has proof that you lied, and that only he can stop you, and that for the good of the people you must be destroyed."

Michael didn't answer. He was no longer surprised.

Jacob looked up at him sadly, but with a fire in his eye. "Sir, I wish I didn't have to tell you. I wish you hadn't heard it from me."

Michael nodded grimly as he lifted his hand. "I have discussed this with the Father," he answered harshly. "This is what he wants us to do. Go to the traitor. Go secretly, before our other men know. Tell him that he has a choice. He can stay if he wants, or he can choose to depart. If he stays, we will fight him and we will see him destroyed, for his hate is too deep, his betrayals too treacherous, to let him stay any longer in our midst. But he could leave. We'd allow that; he could choose to depart. He can slip away in secret and leave us in peace.

"Now go to him, Jacob, and tell him to leave. He can live somewhere else, far away, by himself, but I don't want to see him in this place anymore. And I will not be patient. He must leave without delay."

"Sir," Jacob answered in a hesitant tone. "I have already told him these things."

Michael lifted his head.

"I saw him this afternoon." Jacob's voice was edged with uncertainty and fear.

"You met with him, Jacob?"

"He came to me, sir."

Michael took a step back. "He came to *you,* Jacob."

"Yes, sir, he did. He asked me to join him. He said he would share his power with me. I told him to leave, then came directly to you."

Michael frowned wearily. He knew there was something more. "What else did he tell you, Jacob?" he pressed.

The lieutenant moved toward Michael and lowered his voice. "He said he would stay and fight you. He has sworn to defeat you, to destroy both you and Jehovah. That's all he seems to care about. It's all he thinks about now."

Michael looked away.

He should have listened to the Father. There was no way he could save him, and he shouldn't have tried.

Now look at the price they had paid, the treachery and deceit. How many of his brothers and sisters had already fallen under his spell! It was too high a price, paid in corruption and lost innocence.

"You know, sir," Jacob concluded, recognizing the uncertainty in Michael's eye. "It would be a mistake to underestimate his support. He believes he is rising. And he really thinks he can win."

chapter two

The nursery was a mass of color, motion, and noise, a most pleasant chaos, heartwarming and cheerful, the happy commotion that could be generated only by a group of exquisitely cheerful children. There were twelve in all, of various ages, each of them commanding attention with their irresistible smiles, all of them asking and pointing and laughing and squealing.

The two young adults, frazzled but clearly satisfied, stood above the commotion, a few feet over the small children's heads. They shot a knowing look at each other, and the young woman smiled. "Isn't this great!" she said above the sound of laughter. The young man faked a quick look of exasperation, but then nodded eagerly. He felt a push against his knee as a little boy grabbed his leg, and he fell back in exaggerated motions to roll with him on the soft floor. The young woman, Elizabeth, had to laugh as she watched her brother. He could pretend he was too old for such stuff, but the truth was this was his element, not the university, not his work or his studies. This was where he was comfortable, where he felt most at ease.

She watched him a long moment as he rolled and played with the little boy. "Luke, you enjoy this far too much," she said when he glanced up at her.

"What? This is work, Beth! It's just our calling, you know."

Elizabeth shook her head, knowing that wasn't true. The truth was, though she and her brother had been asked to assist in the nursery, both of them would have volunteered anyway. The little time they spent there, the little attention it took away from their studies and friends, was much more than worth the sacrifice.

She turned and looked down, feeling a tug on her dress. Kneeling, she looked a young girl in the eyes.

"Elizabeth," the little girl said, pronouncing her name with careful effort. "I *really* need to talk to you." The worry on the child's face was unmistakably clear.

Elizabeth, dark-haired and dark-eyed, took the little girl by the hand, walked to a small chair, sat, and pulled her onto her lap, breathing the smell of the child, the soft scent of her skin and thin hair. The girl nestled against her lap and was quiet for a moment. Beth was wearing a slender white dress with a thin blue belt. On her left shoulder, she had pinned a homemade corsage, a mix of wildflowers she had picked from her own garden and fashioned around a white and blue bow. As the little girl climbed higher onto her lap, she leaned against the corsage, crushing it against Beth's chest. Feeling the flowers on her back, the little girl turned and touched the delicate petals, pulling one away.

"What is it, Libby?" Elizabeth asked as the child picked at her corsage.

The little girl's eyes grew more worried. "I have a *really* big problem. And I have prayed and prayed, but I *still* don't know what to do!"

"What is it, baby? Tell me. Let me help."

The child turned shyly away. "I don't know if I should tell you. I know you have a lot to worry about already. Homework. Getting dressed in the mornings. And combing your hair. My mother does all that for me. But who takes care of you?"

Beth quickly suppressed a laugh, for the look on Libby's face made it clear this was no laughing matter. "I'm okay, Libby," she answered in the voice that adults save for sweet little girls. "When you get older, things come a little easier, and you learn to take care of yourself. So don't you worry about me. Now tell me, what's on your mind."

An intense look of worry returned to the child's eyes. Hesitating, she looked away, and Beth pulled her close. "Come on, Libby," she prodded. "You can tell me. I promise you, I can help."

The child turned back toward her and straightened her shoulders, seemingly coming to a decision. "All right," she said. "But promise you won't get mad?"

Beth lifted her hand solemnly to her heart. "I promise," she said. The little girl took a deep breath. "I don't know what kind of pet I should try to have when I'm on earth," she said.

"Oh, my," Beth replied in a very serious tone. "That *is* a big problem. And you say you've prayed about it already."

"Oh, yes. Many, many nights!"

"Okay, then—well, when are you being born?" Beth asked.

The little girl looked around conspiratorially, then reached up and whispered in her ear. Beth pulled away and smiled. "That's still a long, long time away," she offered comfortingly.

"But I *need* to know. We need to make plans, remember?"

Beth nodded in agreement. "Yes, of course you do."

"Do you think . . . ?" the little girl's voice trailed off. "Do you think Father doesn't think it's important? That he doesn't really care?"

"Oh, no, Libby. He knows and he cares. Nothing is unimportant to him. He knows, and he loves you more than you could possibly understand. He knows all our worries. And he will answer you."

Libby nodded. "Okay, then. I'm going to ask him again when I talk to him tonight."

"You should do that. And I promise if you ask him, he will answer you."

The girl smiled, satisfied, then jumped off Beth's lap to join a new game on the floor. Beth watched, then stood up to see Luke staring at her. He nodded to her corsage, which was smashed, the flowers wilting, the bow crushed into a flattened loop. "Too bad," he said.

Elizabeth glanced down and shrugged. "That's okay. I don't mind."

"One day we'll be released and you won't have to worry about little children crushing your flowers."

Beth's face turned thoughtful. "That will be a very sad day for me. Believe me, I will miss my crushed flowers."

Luke reached down to tussle a passing head, then folded his arms and glanced toward the door. "Where is Ammon?" he asked in a serious tone.

Beth's face clouded over. Ammon, their older brother, was supposed to be there with them. "I don't know," she answered. "It's not like him just to not show up."

Luke looked a little worried. He had heard the rumors; they swirled everywhere. Betrayal. Upheaval. Whispers of war. And if that were the case, Ammon would be in the thick of it all. He wouldn't stand by; Luke knew that for certain. Some men, even from the time they were young, had a predisposition for the romance and brotherhood that surrounded a conflict. Some men were just more able to see things in black and white, more willing to step forward and defend those who wouldn't defend themselves.

Ammon was like that, and it had Luke concerned. He thought a moment, then leaned toward Beth. "You know what I heard," he said. Beth turned toward him and shook her head. "Lucifer has come out against Michael . . . "

Beth felt his presence even before she turned around, for there was something in his spirit that seemed to fill the whole room. She turned. The door was open, and Ammon was standing there. She stared at her brother. He looked so handsome, so strong. Deep black eyes, broad shoulders, thin waist, and strong arms. He was tall and masculine, with huge hands and large feet, almost like a puppy that had more room to grow.

Ammon nodded quickly to his younger brother and sister, then turned his eyes on the children. "Hey," he cried. "Big Bear is here!" Half a dozen children looked up and squealed in delight. Throwing their playthings aside, they ran into his arms. He bent down to their level, feeling the drooling kisses on his cheek, then stood as three children attached themselves to each leg, wrapping their tiny arms around his knees while fighting for position over his feet. He laughed and walked forward, lifting them up with each step. He bent at the waist to allow a couple more children to grab onto his arms, and he lifted them too, suspending them in the air. They laughed and kicked their legs, holding on for dear life. More children piled on, pulling on his legs, and he finally fell over, gently rolling with them on the floor.

Beth watched, waiting for Ammon to extract himself from the pile, which he did very quickly, pushing himself to his feet. "Just a minute," he said to the children as he approached Beth and Luke, an apologetic look on his face. “I’m sorry,” he said. “I got hung up. Should have let you know.”

“It’s okay,” Beth said quickly. “We got along okay. The kids miss you more than we do.”

“Where have you been?” Luke asked.

Ammon turned serious, and he pulled his brother and sister aside. “Have you seen Samuel?” he asked them.

They glanced quickly at each other and shook their heads no. “I haven’t seen him for a couple of days,” Beth replied.

Ammon looked away, and she took a worried step forward. “What is it?” she asked him. “What’s going on? What do you know about him?” Their older brother, Sam, had lately become secretive and unapproachable; he never talked to them anymore.

Ammon was silent.

“Ammon,” Beth whispered, “you don’t think Sam’s considering . . . ?” She brought her hand to her mouth.

Ammon thought a long moment, then shook his head no. “It’s probably nothing,” he answered. “I’m sure that Sam will be fine.”

* * *

Samuel, the oldest brother, stood on the edge of the field, looking out on the golden heads, an ocean of bronze swaying in the afternoon sun. He watched the wind blow across the stalks, swirling the wheat, creating ripples and waves as if it were the sea. A sudden gust blew, bending the grain violently. He reached out, palm down, letting the tassels move against his hand.

This was his field. This was his love. It was his peace and his kingdom, where he felt most at home.

He frowned and took a deep breath. It was time that he

go. He thought of his younger brothers and sister. How could they ever understand?

Yes, he would miss them. But he had no choice now.

It was time that he left them. His decision was made.

* * *

Two days later, Ammon and Elizabeth huddled in the main room of their home. The enormous house was empty, and the wind blew gently outside. "Tell me what he said," Ammon insisted again.

Beth hesitated; then, her voice trembling, she spoke quietly. "He said he was leaving. He said that he had to go, and that he was leaving this afternoon."

Ammon sat back and huffed in frustration. "Just like that? Nothing more?"

"No, Ammon. I'm sorry. He packed a few things very quickly, but he didn't take very much."

The young man shook his head. "Didn't he see anyone . . . didn't he speak to anyone else?"

The girl looked away sadly. "No, Ammon. He came and went very quickly. A couple other men were with him. I don't know who they were. They looked like—I don't know—they were dressed differently from anyone I have ever seen. He left with them quickly. And he didn't talk to anyone. I was the only one here."

She pressed her lips tightly. He had planned it that way. It was painfully obvious—but she wasn't going to say anything, not yet, not to Ammon. The fact that Samuel didn't want to say good-bye to his brothers, that he had planned his exit so as not to see Ammon and Luke . . . well, it said a great deal about what was important to him now.

"Did he say anything else?" Ammon pressed. "Did he say when he'd be back?"

She shook her head, then shuddered, almost as if she had experienced a sudden, great pain. Ammon watched her carefully, then leaned toward her, his eyes wide and intense. "Please, Elizabeth, tell me. What did our brother say?"

She shuddered again. She could not lie; it was not in her nature. She was more likely to sprout wings and fly than to deceive him intentionally. And yet it was clearly so painful, so horribly painful for her to think of what Sam had said. She bit on her lip and lowered her eyes. Ammon leaned toward her until their foreheads barely touched. "Please, Elizabeth," he begged her again. "Please tell me what he said."

"He said to tell you . . . " She paused and swallowed again. "He said to tell you not to worry. And not to think about him anymore."

Ammon staggered back and shook his head in disbelief. She looked at him closely, staring into his eyes. He knew. She saw it. He knew the truth too.

"He's not coming back, Ammon," she whispered. "And you've got to find the courage, somehow, to tell Luke."

"It will kill him," Ammon muttered. "He won't understand why his big brother left."

"Luke loves you, Ammon, as much as he ever loved Sam. You have to stay strong for Luke; he will be counting on you."

The young man fell into the nearest chair, his shoulders slumping as if the very breath had slipped out of him. "What is happening?" he cried as he clenched his arms at his chest. "Why is this happening? I just don't understand anymore."

chapter three

Several days later, Ammon found himself on a mountain, climbing away from the city to get some time by himself.

It was the most beautiful place under heaven or sky. Mountains and rock, trees, desert, and blue lake—all lay before him in exquisite detail. The air was so clear he felt he could see the end of the earth, the sky so deep blue, it seemed to merge into space. The view was entirely indescribable to those who were unwilling to pay the price, those unwilling to get out and make the steep mountain climb.

Ammon paused near the top of the mountain and glanced over his shoulder, looking down on the narrow, rocky trail, then turned back to the mountain and, moving surely, pulled himself up through the rocks. He pressed against the mountain, searching for footholds while stretching his fingers across tiny ledges of rock. The sun was at his shoulder and the surface of the rocks was warm to the touch, though there was a coldness that seemed to emanate from deep in the mountain, a chill he could feel when he pressed against the stone, as if the sun's heat didn't penetrate as deeply as it once had.

The seasons were changing. There was great change in the air.

Breathing deeply, the man pulled himself through a small crevice, climbing carefully, and emerged on the top of the highest peak. Stepping away from the ledge, he turned and looked down, following the hidden trail with his eyes as it wound through the trees, then up the side of the mountain. Here and there, the trail completely disappeared, concealed by huge chunks of the mountain. So far as Ammon could tell, he was the only person who knew about the ancient trail; he had never seen anyone on it, and there were no indications of other use. He liked that. In this world it was difficult to keep something like that to oneself.

Turning slowly, near the ledge, Ammon took in the view. To his left and his right, the great mountain range spread for hundreds of miles, craggy fingers of great rock shining in the afternoon sun. The rocky peak on which he stood fell away on two sides, forming sheer cliffs that extended almost to the valley floor. A narrow box canyon wound into the south side of the cliffs. The only vegetation on the mountain peak was the small leaches that grew in between the rock crevices and thin patches of wire grass that struggled through the rough soil. There were no trees or shrubs on this side of the mountain, for he was right at the tree line where the snow stayed until midsummer and the wind always blew. Just behind him, however, on the gently sloping face, was a forest of incredible trees, massive green firs with wide, spreading bows, ancient as the rivers, splendid and tall. The trees swayed like an ocean in the afternoon breeze. If he listened carefully, Ammon could hear the powerful *whoosh* of the wind moving through the trees, the sound echoing off the mountain walls and rising on the wind. He took a deep breath, the scent was sweet and musky with pine. He savored the silence. It was good to be alone. It was worth the long climb just to be by himself, to have time to ponder and say his simple prayers.

Looking out on the landscape, familiar words came to his mind. *This is holy ground.* Standing on top of the mountain, he always felt the same way.

What was it, he wondered, that drove him to the summit? What was it that compelled him to climb the steep path, working his way up the dangerous trail? He couldn't answer the question; all he knew was that he felt it necessary to climb, to reach the highest point, to be on top of the world, to measure the distance, to see both sides of the mountain and the granite peaks all around. Being up there helped him, somehow, to understand the way things operated down below, reminding him that there was more to life than the day-to-day grind.

Below the magnificent trees, the great city spread in every direction. On the other side of the city, far in the distance, the shallow lake reflected the afternoon light, a huge bowl of white sand holding a splash of pure blue. The city center was breathtaking, with vertical buildings of white granite and gray limestone reaching up to the sky. Beautiful homes, each a lesson in exquisite architecture, spread from the downtown area to the base of the mountain and west to the lake, reaching almost to the shore. The city was alive with people moving through the afternoon rush. He knew that, even as he watched, somewhere down there in the tallest buildings, Michael and his leaders were meeting to draw up their plans. Elizabeth was down there too, and Luke. And the enemy was down there, also making his plans.

Ammon sat and leaned his head against the rock, then lowered his head and slowly closed his eyes. He listened to the wind moving through the tall trees and felt the heat of the sun and the cool mountain air. In a world of growing contention, he needed this time. He needed time to think about Samuel and why his brother had left.

* * *

As Ammon sat in thought, believing he was alone, the other man kept his distance, watching carefully through a gap in the trees.

As the sun dropped to the horizon, Ammon heard footsteps, the sound of soft leather soles crossing the rocks. He stood and turned quickly. The man moved toward him, approaching from behind, his face hidden by shadow and a low-hanging tree. He was short and dark haired, a plug of a man, imposing by his thickness, determined and bullish, with a broad neck and thick arms. He marched up the sloping side of the mountain with deliberate strides, then forced a broad smile and extended his hand.

Ammon moved toward him, and the two men embraced. "Ammon, I knew I'd find you," the other man said.

"Master Balaam," Ammon answered, "what are you doing here?"

Balaam held Ammon by the shoulders and stared into his eyes. "It's good to see you, Ammon."

"Thank you," Ammon answered. He studied his former teacher. "You look well, Master Balaam."

Balaam frowned and shook his head. "Don't waste the politeness on me, Ammon. I know how I look. I look worried. And tired. And I feel even worse."

"Why is that, Balaam?"

The great teacher didn't answer as he walked a few steps away.

Balaam was older than Ammon, his face a little more worn, his hands a little more rough, though there was not a full generation that separated the men. He was the chancellor at the main university, the headmaster, as he was known, and for many years Balaam had been one of Ammon's favorite instructors. Demanding and intelligent, a bit on the fringe, eccentric and emotional, Master Balaam was loved by his students and respected by his peers. He filled his entire classroom with the booming sound of his voice, sometimes rising, sometimes falling, emotion and drama seeming to carry every word. Some said he was melodramatic, and there was no doubt that was true, but he loved teaching and the classroom, for it was his stage and he was always the star.

Ammon patted Balaam happily on the shoulders, then took a step back. "Balaam, how have you been?" he asked. "It has been a long time."

"Yes, a long time. I am fine; thank you for asking. And how is my star pupil? I always hear good things about you."

Ammon smiled awkwardly as he settled himself on the flat rock. The afternoon sun bathed them in a warm light, but it was setting very quickly and a cool evening breeze was beginning to blow. Balaam placed his hands on his hips and took Ammon in; always the professor, he measured his charge.

In a city of beautiful people, Ammon was one of the most beautiful. His light hair blew back and fell over his neck, and his ice-cold blue eyes were piercing and bright. His face was square; he was tall; his grip was bone-crushingly tight. He came from a good family; there was no doubt about that. *Ammon* was a good name; it had deep roots and strength. It meant courage and daring. *Son of the Light.*

Yes, *Ammon* was a good name. And they needed this man. He had incredible potential, with his courage and strength. He was just what they needed. And Balaam had been sent for him.

But he's so young, Balaam thought. *So young and naïve.* He studied his friend from behind a blank mask. He thought it was too early, that they were pushing too hard. They needed to give life more time to steal the zest out of him, more time to frustrate him with disappointments and regrets.

He puzzled a moment. Perhaps he should wait.

No! He had his instructions. It had to be now.

Balaam studied his former student, and Ammon became uncomfortable as the silence grew long. He scraped the ground with his foot. "Where have you been, Balaam?" he asked. "I heard you were out of town."

Balaam folded his arms. "Oh, you know, we teachers have to get away and recharge every once in a while."

"Sabbatical?"

"Of sorts."

"You've been gone a long time."

"Long enough to see that much has changed since I left."

Ammon grunted in agreement, then stared at his friend. "Balaam, why are you here?" he finally asked.

"I wanted to talk to you, Ammon."

"You couldn't just come by my home?"

"I wanted to see you alone. Someplace where we could talk for a while without being interrupted. And I know what it's like at your place. I've been there—remember? It's like a carnival. Music. Dancing. And far too much singing! Your place is so noisy, it hurts my ears."

Ammon smiled. "You'll have to talk to my sister; she's responsible for that. She has more friends, I believe, than anyone else I know."

"How is Elizabeth doing?"

"She's gorgeous and happy. Just what you would expect."

Balaam nodded. "And Sam?" he asked, though he already knew.

Ammon didn't answer. Balaam waited a moment, then let the question pass.

Ammon stared across the valley and the falling light. "You didn't hike up the ancient trail, I suppose?" he asked as he nodded toward the cliffs at his feet.

Balaam almost snorted. "Of course not," he huffed. "Only a fool would climb the old trail." He gestured toward the back side of the mountain and its gentle slope. "There are more reasonable ways, much easier ways, to get up here."

"Other ways, yes, but they aren't as interesting."

Balaam picked up a sharp rock and ran his finger along the edge, feeling its hardness, stroking it carefully. "So let me see," he said with almost a tease in his voice. "Since I have been gone you completed your studies and graduated top of your class. Chairman of the student committee. A gifted musician. A fierce, almost heartless, competitor on the field. I swear, Ammon, you are the most ambitious student I have ever known."

"Ambitious?" Ammon questioned. "I don't know about that. Some things come to me easily; other things I have to work at very hard."

As he talked, Ammon thought of the last test he had taken before summer break at the university, an oral examination with one of the department heads, a cranky and unpleasant fellow with eyebrows that extended like a barn owl's ears. What had been scheduled for a half day spilled through the afternoon and into the night, turning a normal evaluation into a grueling and nerve-racking ordeal, a contest of wills, a battle to prove how much Ammon *really* knew. The examination crossed subjects and specialties, delving into issues of philosophy and moral character. Ammon had a reputation as an intelligent student and gifted athlete as well, and the professor was convinced this had to be a mistake. By the time it was over, Ammon was nearly sick with exhaustion. Yet he had answered every question, and he felt a quiet thrill. Standing at the desk, he watched the professor write one simple line in his notes: *Ammon has completed the examination in a satisfactory manner.*

High praise, indeed. And Ammon couldn't have been more relieved.

Thinking of the experience, he couldn't help but smile. Ambitious! Hardly. But he wasn't afraid to go toe-to-toe with a professor, not when he called him out, hoping to prove that he was less than he was. Ammon considered the experience, then turned to Balaam and said, "No, sir, I don't think I'm so ambitious, and I know I'm not as talented or as smart as most. I just seem a little more confident, maybe because I'm willing to work a little harder than they do."

Balaam listened, then shrugged. "All right then, a minor distinction. But for whatever reason, you seem to continue to do very well."

"Maybe. Thanks for noticing. But I don't suppose you came all the way up the mountain just to tell me I do a good job?"

"That, and to take in the view."

Ammon laughed pleasantly. He knew that wasn't true. Balaam didn't live slowly. He didn't "take in the view." His life was lived at full speed: *"Listen to me! Learn! Or get out of my class! Don't talk to me about beauty. I'm teaching reality here!"* The teacher was far too intense to stop and smell the roses. The only occasion when he might catch the scent of a flower was when he cut through the gardens on his way to a meeting or some other activity that was worth his valuable time.

Ammon glanced down at the trail and smiled. Balaam out hiking? To take in the view? It was just about as likely that the sun would fall from the sky. "Tell you what," Ammon challenged as he patted a rock. "Come, then. Sit down. The sun is just going down. We can watch the sunset together while you *take in the view*."

Balaam swallowed, but he nodded and sat down heavily. He looked immediately frustrated. He liked to move when he talked, to illustrate with his hands and express himself with broad gestures that gave life to his words. Still, he sat down on a flat rock near the edge of the cliff and stared into space, looking over the city below. "Ammon, can I speak with you frankly?" he asked after a time.

"Has it ever been otherwise?"

Balaam slowly nodded. Yes, there had been times.

Ammon leaned slightly forward. He had seen the nod. "What's on your mind, Balaam?" he asked hesitantly.

The teacher fidgeted a moment, then stood up and walked to the edge of the ledge and searched the horizon. The sun was starting to dip, burning through the low sky, turning from an indefinable brightness to a deep reddish hue.

"War is coming," Balaam said. "It is coming, I know. I don't think you believe it. A civil war, here! But it is coming, I tell you, and others know it's coming too."

Ammon answered slowly. "Maybe. We'll see. But there are still many leaders who believe that it won't come to that."

Balaam frowned deeply. "They do not understand."

Ammon studied his teacher. "Do *you* understand, Balaam? What makes you so sure?"

"Listen to me, Ammon," he answered in a low voice. "The pressure is building. Like an overfilled balloon, it is waiting to burst. Everyone feels the strain; there's no way it can hold. There are too many misunderstandings and too much jealousy, too many hurt feelings and too much hate to keep in. And when the war breaks, it won't be subtle. It will be sudden and brutal, with enormous casualties. Women and children, the young and the old—all will be victims in the coming war. It will be a war of attrition, not a battle for ground. It will be a war whose only purpose is to inflict casualties. It will be winner take all and the spoils not divided until the battle is through. No one will be safe. All will feel this war's pain."

Balaam paused, then swept his arms across the enormous horizon. "The battle draws near. Like a storm cloud in the evening sky, the conflict looms large—dark, mean, and boiling with thunder and light. And though the coming storm is out there for everyone to see, because it is off in the distance, and because of its size, some find it impossible to gauge how close it really is. Is it moving toward us? Is it moving away? Some people wonder. Some people still hope. Perhaps it will pass. Perhaps it will blow itself out. But I'm telling you, Ammon, this storm will not veer away. It is approaching, and quickly. A dark night draws near.

"And there is only one way to avoid the disaster that is coming, only one way to avoid the destruction of all."

Ammon shook his head as he looked out on the city and the blue lake beyond. He thought a long moment, suddenly sad.

In that instant he saw a vision . . . no, he felt a vision, for it was much more a feeling than something he could see with his eyes. It was as if he were looking on something that had already occurred, looking back on a memory that had already been, something he had seen, even experienced, though a long time ago. Fuzzy and soft-edged, he saw the vision unfold.

The great city lay empty. All of the people were gone. It was a canyon of brick and marble, empty, narrow, and deep. A dry wind blew down a long, lonely street, pushing paper and dust through a half-open door. A single bird, black and ugly, lay motionless in the street. All was quiet. And there was a smell in the air like nothing he had ever smelled before. The air was thick, brown, and gritty, and it was growing dark.

And the city was empty!

Where had everyone gone?

Millions of people! No! Even more . . . !

A deep shiver ran through him, and his skin seemed to crawl. He shook his head to clear it and pulled in his arms.

War! In this place! How could it ever be? The word was so rarely spoken it just didn't fit here. It was simply inconceivable that war would come to their homes. It had happened in *other* places, true, but that was a long time before and a long way away. This place was special, this place was *home,* battles took place *over there,* not in their backyards.

And yet Ammon knew that Balaam was right.

The most terrifying element of the coming war, and the thing that made it so easy to deny, was the fact that the rot had grown from the inside and was already bone-deep. Home had a cancer. Home had a disease. Home had an ugly, hidden virus, putrid and deadly and capable of bringing their entire society down. Evil people, hiding behind the right of expression, had joined forces and plotted to bring their freedoms to an end. And those people walked in their midst, smiling and plotting and hating their friends, while waiting for the day when they could fight in the open instead of slink in the dark, their jealousy and hate quietly boiling inside. For them it was no longer a question of what was right or what was wrong, only of which feelings had control of their hearts: the love they had felt for each other and their God, or the hate that now stewed because of their jealous pride.

Yes, war was coming. It fact, it was already here.

Ammon didn't move as he thought, taking in a deep breath of night air. He shook his head again, looked at Balaam, then stood at his side. The sun had slipped below the horizon, leaving the western sky a deep pink. Behind him, the moon was just beginning to rise. It was white now, not yellow, a sliver of pale light.

"I guess the battle continues," Ammon said.

Balaam raised an eyebrow. "What do you mean?"

"The forces of good and evil have been in conflict since the beginning of time, since the heavens were formed, since we first took breath. And this is no different. It's all the same struggle, though in a different time, different place. Dark clouds and dark feelings. Yes, the war clouds are near."

Balaam studied his student with a critical eye. "Ammon," he asked. "Do you know who will win?"

Ammon didn't hesitate. "There is no doubt in my mind."

"Then are you ready to join us?"

Ammon turned away from his friend.

chapter four

Ammon and Balaam talked until darkness settled over the mountain, their quiet voices rising and falling in the night wind. A gust of cool air blew up from the valley, musky with scent, and the moon rose behind them, providing a shimmer of light that cast a dim shadow on the valley below. As night grew deeper, the stars grew more intense and the wind suddenly became calm, the air heavy, like a blanket, brooding and thick. The two men stood close together, their voices suddenly intense. Ammon grew angry. Balaam hissed in reply. Lifting his fist, he tapped his friend on the chest. Ammon pushed back, then walked away furiously. The teacher called him back with a simple command. They talked a little longer, Ammon shaking his head, and then the two parted quickly, moving along separate trails.

As Ammon walked down the path that led off the back side of the mountain, he paused and looked back. How could this happen? he wondered. He needed to know. One of the great teachers! One of the most respected individuals he knew, a man who influenced a thousand students each day. He swallowed and called out, but the teacher didn't slow. "Balaam," he shouted again through a dry mouth. Master Balaam slowed and looked back, his eyes seeming to glint in the light. He stood there, impatient, obviously anxious to go. There was no more use talking; it was only wasting his time. He scowled, then turned quickly and disappeared down the trail.

As Ammon watched, a great sense of darkness washed over him. Had the whole world gone crazy? Was there no one he could trust?

* * *

Balaam entered his house. It was gloomy and quiet, for none of the lights were turned on. He walked down the dark hallway, tossing his outer cloak on the rack.

A shadow was waiting for him in the darkness, anxious and impatient, his arms folded across his chest. The man watched Balaam closely, his breathing even and slow. Balaam started when he saw him, almost stumbling back. He gasped, then, embarrassed, quickly turned on the light.

The man looked up and smiled with a fiendish grin, mischievous, almost hateful, alive and intense. He leaned forward, always eager, as if he were ready to pounce, prepared to find insult, prepared to offend. "I frightened you," he offered in his great and powerful voice.

Balaam replied weakly as he glanced at the floor. "Yes, sir. I didn't expect to see you here tonight."

The intruder laughed lightly as a wonderful shiver moved through his bones. Fear! Yes, they feared him! Even his friends. He laughed once again, then commanded, "Turn the light off."

Balaam hesitated, and the stranger waved to the light with his hand. "The moon is high now. It will provide enough light. Let's sit in the darkness and enjoy the night. The dark is more intimate. The dark is for friends. It takes away inhibitions. And I want you to be open with me."

Balaam sensed the burning eyes and felt a black chill. He did as he was told, then moved to the table and nervously pulled out a chair. As he sat, he bowed slightly, a nearly imperceptible drop of his head. He glanced at his visitor, then looked quickly away.

The man sat in the shadows, his face an unfeeling mask, handsome, even striking, his features rugged and lean. But a spider web of creases now ran from the corners of his eyes, and the brow on his forehead was furrowed by deeply cut lines. A thin line of silver-gray ran through the center of his hair, an otherwise beautiful mane of jet-black which hung to the back of his neck. As always, his hair was tied back with a deep purple bow. He had a masculine face, angry and unpredictable. His eyes were pale and piercing and incredibly intense, questioning and suspicious behind a dark stare. His fingers were long, even elegant, though mortal age, if it came, would make them bony and weak. He wore a simple gray robe tied with a red sash.

If there was one word to describe him, that word would have been *cold*. Cold skin, cold hands, cold smile, and cold heart. He was a bitter winter morning; ice chips ran through his veins. Like an exquisite ice sculpture, yes, there was beauty there; but there was nothing in his presence that invited an embrace. To hold him, to touch him, was to bring a cold chill, for there was no warmth left inside him, no kindness at all. Like a dead, dried-out insect, he had a hard, brittle shell, but inside he was empty except for his hate.

Over the years, the man had taken on several names, some respectful, some offensive, some old and some new. In the old days, long before, they had called him *Son of the Morning*, but he hated that name now from the depths of his soul. The connotation was insulting; he just didn't buy any of it anymore. After Son of the Morning, he had been assigned other names: Rahab, the Deceiver, the Father of Lies, Destroyer, the Betrayer, Slanderer, and Adversary.

He was sometimes called Master Mahan, but only by his closest and most secret friends, and then only in whispers, and always in the dark, when the angels weren't watching and the wind wouldn't carry the name. All of the others around him, those who fell under his spell, called him Lucifer or Satan.

At this point in his life, in the premortal world, Lucifer was still a great prince, a spirit of incredible power, a leader among those who were still seeking their way. But the truth was that he had already fallen, though few fully knew his heart and what he ultimately intended to do.

The great leader was rising, his star shining bright, for he had developed a scheme, a much easier way. Many believed him. And he was spreading the word.

chapter five

Lucifer sat back and looked Balaam in the eye, then placed his hands on the table. "So . . . ?" he asked intently. "What did he say?"

Balaam hesitated, then answered, "He told me no."

Lucifer snorted in disgust. "We need him," he cried.

"There are others, master."

"Yes, there are others. And I want them all—the weak for their weakness and the strong for their strength. Every one of them is important. Haven't I made myself clear? If we don't defeat them here, we will have to fight them again. And I don't want to do that. I want to take them all now!"

"But there are so many children. Do you expect to approach every one?"

"Yes! Absolutely! We will go after them all! There is not a single individual I don't want on my side. Each of them is worth our effort, each is worth our time, especially these warriors, these brave, valiant ones. They have so much power, and they are so strong. They are godlike in spirit, and they will be powerful! So we need to defeat them before they can see, before they understand their potential and what they can be, before they can learn how to defeat me, before they learn what I know.

"So, yes, Balaam, I intend to go after them all. The battle is looming . . . no, the battle is here; it began on the day they rejected my views. And the first thing we must do is to destroy their leaders, for Elohim and Jehovah are counting on them. If I cut out their leaders, they grow weak and I grow strong. For every leader I convert, we bring a thousand to our side; for once we have their leaders, we can send them into the world to convert their family and friends.

"And though Ammon is young, he has much to give. He could lead an entire division, ten thousand strong."

Balaam nodded slowly, his face tight with concern. The conversation with Ammon had left him frustrated and tense, and a simmer of doubt pulled his gut into a tight ball of nerves. "And if we can't get Ammon?" he asked slowly.

Lucifer scowled. "I gave you an assignment, Balaam. You ought not let me down."

"But, sir, as you said, Ammon is young but he's strong. And my discussion with him, it didn't go well."

Lucifer leaned angrily across the table. "I will be very disappointed if you can't get Ammon," he said. "That would force me to reevaluate my offer and what worth you might be to me."

Balaam fell back, a look of despair in his eyes.

Lucifer tapped the table. "If we can't get Ammon to join us, we will go after his younger brother instead. Luke is loyal, but naïve, malleable, and bent by the wind. I can win him; I know that. Then I'll turn him against Ammon. We might not get everything, but either way, we will win."

Balaam paused and glanced down, a look of doubt in his eyes. Battles were rarely that easy when it came to men's souls, and he needed reassurance. "But, master," he questioned, "how do you know? It mightn't be that easy. How can you be so sure?"

Lucifer stood abruptly, his eyes flashing bright, the façade of his smile twisted into a tight frown. The rage that simmered inside him seemed to boil over. "Don't question me, Balaam!" he said in a snarl. "There are things I can do, unspeakable things, torments so exquisite you will wish you *could* die. So don't question me, Balaam. Keep your doubts to yourself. If you can't be strong when I need you, then get out of my way."

The teacher pulled back, his eyes wide open in fear. "I didn't mean to question," he sniffled in pain. "I just wonder, dear master, how it is that you know."

Lucifer cut him off with a furious wave of his hand. "*I know I'm not like Him!*" he hissed in rage. "I'm not perfect. I can't see the future like the Father can. But I do know his children. Since the beginning of time, I have studied them every day. I know how they think. I know how they feel. I know what they hope for and what they really want. And I can always predict how they are going to react. And though all people are different—*and oh, how they glory in their diversity!*—they have one thing in common, and I am a master at that. Pride is the seed from which all other sins sprout: jealousy, hate, lust, ambition, criticism, or sloth. All of these sins sprout from the pride in their hearts. If I can breed pride inside them, I can turn that pride into hate. Once I have made them feel jealous, then I can bend them to follow my will.

"So even though I can't *see* the future, not like Him anyway, I can still predict the future with comfortable certainty. And I can promise you, Balaam, that many, no . . . most of His children will end up on my side, all of the weak and even many of the strong. It won't happen today and it won't happen next week, but I will defeat them; I promise you I will. As long as the Father and the Christ continue to guarantee their agency, something their laws seem to have bound them to do, then we can manipulate His children to steal them away. And if we control enough of His children, if we pull enough to our side, then we can cast out the Father and His precious Son, cast them out into darkness and eternal woe."

Balaam shivered lightly as a cold chill ran down his spine. *Yes, they could do it. His master was right!*

"And remember," Lucifer added, as he narrowed his eyes, "this battle we are starting will never end. We have an eternity to destroy them, and time is on our side. This isn't a quick skirmish that will be resolved in one fight. It will go on and on, until we say it is over or until we have won. Remember that, Balaam. We choose our battles. We choose our terms!"

"Yes!" Balaam answered, his eyes burning with excitement, even in the dim light.

Lucifer moved around the table, his face pale and tight. "I want Ammon," he hissed in a low, lusty voice. "I want Ammon. And the girl. Elizabeth is a part of my plan. And if we can't convince them to join us, then let's go after Luke. The little brother, the innocent, loved one—what would Ammon do for him? And Elizabeth—how she loves him! Would they sacrifice themselves for this brother? I believe that they would.

"So go. Now! Talk to Luke. I want you to bring him to me."

Balaam nodded solemnly. "Yes, master, I will."

Lucifer smiled, then pointed a bony finger and tapped him on the chest. Turning quickly, he walked from the room, slipping into the darkness and disappearing into the night.

* * *

The argument with Master Balaam had left Ammon feeling agitated and angry. After returning from the mountain, he stood on a wooded pathway near his home and looked over his head, taking in the incredible array of stars. He glanced around, then sat on the grass to watch the night sky. A wisp of cloud passed, carried by the wind, and the night grew more dark as the cloud moved in front of the moon. He listened to the cicadas and the rustling breeze; like the waves on the oceans, the trees rolled and swayed. The grass smelled damp and sweet, and he took a deep breath. For a long time he remained motionless, his thoughts hazy and thick.

He felt restless and weary, anxious in body and soul. He had been agitated for several days, ever since his brother had left, and the conversation with Balaam had only made him feel worse.

He took another deep breath, then lay back on the grass and closed his eyes to the dark.

The dream came unexpectedly, as they all did, though dreams were one of his gifts. The vision stuck in his mind, an image of mortality and what it might be.

* * *

There was a small, white, wooden frame schoolhouse, a two-story building with a bell tower perched atop a wide, wooden porch. The playground was crowded, and the sounds of children playing filled the air.

Ammon saw himself as a child, hopping down the front steps and running through the schoolyard. At the corner of the building he stopped suddenly; his heart jumped in his chest. He saw the group of bullies and was instantly afraid. The group of older boys had formed a tight circle around a much younger child and were jabbing at him, taunting and teasing and calling him names. Ammon watched the assault with a knot in his throat. He shifted his view, but he couldn't see who the young child was. The child tried to push through the circle, and the older boys pushed him back. Other children gathered around, laughing and pointing in scorn. One of the bullies approached an older girl and pulled a pink sweater from her arms. "Put this on!" he sneered as he thrust it toward the young boy. "Come on, little sissy, pink is perfect for you!"

The little boy cried and pushed the sweater away. The older boys howled and the circle drew tight. Ammon stepped to the side, trying to see again who it was, but the little boy's face remained hidden behind his raised arms. "Hey!" Ammon called angrily, and a couple of tormenters turned to face him. He started toward the circle, but the largest boy scowled. "Stay out of this, Ammon, or you'll get the same thing!"

Ammon froze, a stone of fear in his chest. He felt his neck tighten and the air rasp in his chest. He felt his blood boil. It was six against one! Six against one, and a child at that! It was disgusting and cowardly. What had this child ever done? He took another step forward and the ringleader sneered, "Get out of here, Ammon, or I'll take this pink sweater and shove it down your throat."

Ammon tried to walk, but his feet wouldn't move. He tried to call out, but the sound didn't get past his throat. The ringleader glared at him, his lips a crooked sneer. Then, satisfied, he snorted and turned back to the child. Pushing him to the ground, he kicked him once in the back. The little boy rolled on his stomach, and several boys moved forward and draped the pink sweater over him. Then, at some unseen signal, they all turned and ran.

The little boy pushed himself up and held his face in his palms. The dirty sweater draped over his shoulders like an ugly pink cape. As the older boys scattered, Ammon finally moved to his side. He put his arms around him, and the little boy cried. He buried his face on Ammon's shoulder and heaved in great sobs.

Ammon stroked his matted hair as he rocked him back and forth, resting his cheek against the blond curls.

As Ammon held the young boy, something drew his eyes toward the school. He turned and saw a man watching from the window on the second floor. It was clear from his face he had seen the whole thing, for he looked deeply dejected, disappointed and sad. Ammon felt a shudder pass through him as he stared up in shame. The man met his eyes sadly, holding him with his stare.

Ammon had not helped this child, but had frozen in fear. He had stood by, afraid, unwilling to get in the fight. The man shook his head, then turned away from the glass. Ammon closed his eyes and lowered his head in disgrace.

* * *

The shameful dream passed and Ammon found himself staring at the night sky again. He felt the cool darkness around him and the soft grass under his back. His heart pounded inside him, and his throat was bone dry. An overwhelming sadness settled through him, leaving him shaken and weak.

He lay there a long time trying to regain his bearings, while staring blankly at the stars and moon overhead.

The dream left him dejected and full of concern. Was that what earth-life would be like? Why didn't he fight? How could he just stand there? Was he a coward at heart?

He replayed the dream until he couldn't stand it anymore, then pushed himself up from the grass and turned for his home. As he walked he flexed his back and lifted his arms. The tension was growing, making him anxious and tight. Like a thousand strands of steel, the energy screamed through his veins, twisting and building, wanting to burst from inside.

He wanted a body. He wanted to fight! If that was what earth-life would be like, fine. He wouldn't cower or turn his back on the fight. He wouldn't sit on his hands, like he had in this dream. He thought of the matted hair and the little boy's sobs. He thought of the bullies and what they had done. If he saw that on earth, no way would he stand by, no way he would let such an ugly thing go. He would fight for this child, fight anyone, anytime. If his Father was looking for someone who wasn't afraid of a scrap, then he was the one and he was ready to go.

"Just give me a body!" he cried out to the empty air. "Give me something to fight with, and I *will* fight them for you!"

* * *

At about the same time Ammon lay in the darkness looking up at the stars, Balaam stood at his doorway and watched Lucifer slip into the night. He stayed there a long moment, staring at the empty dark and feeling a chill that was not from the cold.

He kept reminding himself what Lucifer had promised at the Great Council. "Not one soul will be lost. Not one single soul!"

And Balaam believed him. He had believed him ever since he had heard the two proposals for how to carry out the Father's plan. It was clear from the beginning which proposal had more potential, which showed more mercy, which demonstrated more love. More importantly, there was so much more *power* in Lucifer's way. Angels and minions would fall at his feet, anxious to do his bidding, knowing their very lives were dependent on his call and whim. Fear and respect, Balaam thought, were greater forces than love, and if they didn't love him, they would respect him still.

And Lucifer had promised from the beginning to share his

power with them. All of his followers would share in his wealth. It wouldn't be hoarded by the Father, as in Jehovah's way.

And though sometimes Balaam wondered if he was on the right track, he was not turning back now. This was his chance to make a real name for himself, to gain the fame and recognition he had been starving for. Forget all that teaching. Where was the glory in that? There was no real distinction, no real power or fame. So he was sticking with Lucifer, no matter the cost.

* * *

After their night meeting, it was a long time before Balaam saw Lucifer again, for the Deceiver quit walking openly among the children of God, finding it difficult to work in the Light. Still, Satan continued his work, passing instructions to his followers through an army of messengers who still worked and lived with them.

Over time, Lucifer took many of his followers and migrated to other parts, to cities far off that could provide a harbor for the rebellious and those who supported him. His people quickly became mischievous and subtle, anxious to protest and find pretext for offense. And though the cities he inhabited were not out of sight (for all things were known unto God), they were far enough away that Lucifer and his followers could be left by themselves, and yet close enough that they could proselyte their rebellion among the children of God.

As their work progressed, Lucifer was very pleased with the result. His angels proved to be defiant and persuasive; indeed, they proved powerful. And they were tireless in their efforts, taking true pleasure in their work. With so many to deceive, so many to bring down, the field was white and their harvest was full.

chapter six

They walked side by side, Luke and Elizabeth, and she slipped her hand easily through his arm. He leaned toward her slightly but did not turn his head. He was quiet, which was unusual, for Luke was generally hard to rattle; high-strung and impetuous, he always had a smile on his face (though Ammon sometimes teased that was only because he wasn't smart enough to realize when things were going wrong). But he was troubled now; she could see that by the distant look in his eye. He was too slow to answer, too slow to laugh, his mind obviously elsewhere as they walked the path through the woods.

The garden was beautiful, with moss-covered rocks, wildflowers, and lush trees reaching a hundred feet over their heads. A pool of clean water, cold and crisp, babbled over the stones, and the heavy scent of lilacs filled the afternoon air. A group of children squeezed by them, racing down the path, laughing in delight as they ran between the adults, brushing their legs as they passed. As the little ones pushed by, Elizabeth smiled, winked to Luke, then chased after them. "Race!" she called out. "First to the river wins!" The children laughed even louder and ran down the grassy path, giggling and screaming with the enthusiasm unique to small children. Beth laughed along with them as she disappeared around a bend in the pathway. Luke quickened his pace, but didn't chase after her.

As Luke approached the cool pond, he found her waiting on a rock, resting, her chin on her knees, looking over the water, where it formed a wide pool. She wore a simple white dress that fit to her calves, and she pulled it tightly around her legs as she sat. The children had left them, racing on to the next great adventure, the sound of their laughter quickly fading away. It was humid and cool, the shade deep and full from the umbrella of trees. The water babbled around them from a small waterfall, and the birds filled the branches with a wonderful sound. The scene was flawless and complete, incomprehensibly perfect. It smelled fresh, like the forest. Beth took a deep breath. "I hope I can remember what it smells like," she said.

"You won't," Luke replied sadly as he moved to her side. "It has to be taken, Beth, all of it taken away."

"Everything?" Elizabeth asked.

"That's what I've been told."

Elizabeth looked out on the pool, then extended her leg and dipped a bare foot in the water, swirling it gently, feeling the cold. "What do you think it will be like?" she asked.

Luke thought a moment, then hunched his shoulders. "It won't be as pretty."

"But do you think it will be close? Could it be almost as wonderful?"

He walked to the edge of the water, which was so clear he could see twenty feet down, to the bottom of the pool. "I don't see how it could be," he answered as he bent down and dipped a single finger into the water.

Beth nodded, unhappily. "I suppose you're right. Worse, our Parents won't be there, and neither will Jehovah." She took another deep breath. The two were silent; then Beth turned quickly, her face suddenly brightened by a wonderful smile, a smile that seemed to emit from somewhere inside her, somewhere from the depths of her soul. Her eyes danced, alive and excited. "But it will still be beautiful, Luke!" she said happily, easily putting her previous questions aside. "It will have to be beautiful, for it will be patterned after this place."

Luke watched her and smiled. She just wouldn't stay down. And her optimism was as captivating as her smile. "I suppose," he answered as he turned from the pool and sat down by her side. "But look around you, Elizabeth. Look anywhere. Everything. Everyplace. It's so perfect. The people, and the beauty of being with Father. Talking face to face with Jehovah, drawing on his experience and listening to him. Being held by the Father and feeling his love. It's too good to remember. The memory has to be taken. It is part of the plan."

Elizabeth nodded slowly. "I wish we could remember *something,*" she said.

"You want to know what I think?" Luke offered. Elizabeth nodded hopefully. "Though it won't be as beautiful," he continued, "I think the earth is going to be a lot like this place. Here there are more sounds and more smells, more color. The music is more perfect, feelings more vibrant, the things we see more intense. The little things are more subtle and the big things more grand. Everything is more powerful and more perfect here. Even love is more perfect, more forgiving and complete.

"But the earth will also be beautiful. And it will be similar, even familiar, because, like you said, it will be patterned after this place. It will be darker, I suppose, even on the best days, even in the most beautiful spots, but it will all be familiar and I think we might know, or at least we might *feel* we have been there before. And I believe we will recognize some places, recognize the same *feelings* of awe that we feel right now. But I suppose it might be like looking out on our world through a thin, wispy veil, a veil that is blowing in the wind, quiet, almost transparent, yet still always there, sheer enough to see through, yet material enough to hide the detail and clarity that we see in this world. The same beauty will be there, but I suspect it will not be as intense. Still, it will be enough to remind us there has to be more, that there is another place, and that we want to return."

Beth nodded, her long hair shaking lightly against her back, then looked around again. "I will miss this place." She moved her head slowly, as if she were trying to memorize the view and then said, "I wish I could capture this scene, that I had the talent to portray this beauty on canvas and oil. But I never could. No matter how much I practice, I could never capture this beauty with paint."

Luke glanced at her hands, seeing the tiny flecks of color on the ends of her fingers and nails. She painted every day. It was one of her goals. "You have gotten very good," he answered. "That last picture you did, the one with the blue and pink pastels, it is as beautiful as anything I have ever seen."

Beth brightened again, her voice suddenly excited. "Do you really think so?" she asked, grabbing hold of his hand.

"No doubt, Beth, no doubt. Ammon had it framed. He's going to put it upstairs in the sunroom. He loves the painting as much as I do."

Beth nodded gratefully, then looked around and said, "Still, I *will* miss this place."

"All of us will. Somewhere deep inside, we will all want to

come home." Reaching down, Luke ran his fingers through the grass, his face suddenly troubled. "It is too perfect here," he said softly. "No worries, no anguish, no fear, our lives conducted in incredible joy. From time immemorial, that's how it's been, time with our family, always making new friends, summer days, winter evenings, all the time in the world. Learning and growing together . . . " His voice dropped to a whisper. "But all that is fading now. It is going away. And it all makes me weary. I don't want things to change."

Beth bit on her lip, then lifted a finger and played nervously with her hair. Luke smiled at the action, knowing she was in deep thought. "I think you hit on the key," she said after a moment of silence. Luke looked at her, puzzled. "Think of what you said," she explained. "*Learning and growing*. That's what we've been doing together. And now we've progressed to the point where that has to change. We can't progress any longer in this estate. And though we've been happy, we've never felt perfect joy. For that, we need to be tested, we need to grow. We need to attain physical bodies and become like God.

"So yes, it is fading, things are changing, that's true. And in the coming process, we are going to have to feel pain."

"If you ask me, pain is overrated," Luke joked. But he hardly smiled.

Beth knew he was only half kidding, and it worried her. She folded her arms in her lap. "Luke," she asked quietly, "can I ask you something? Something personal? And will you be honest with me?"

Luke turned to face her. "Of course, Beth. You know that you can."

She stared at her hands, adjusting them in her lap. "Are you ever frightened?" she asked. "Are you afraid of being born?" She lifted her eyes and looked at him anxiously.

Luke stared across the water and furrowed his brow. Was he afraid? He didn't really know. At what point did uncertainty cross the line into fear? "I guess I'm a little scared of the pain and the darkness that accompany birth," he answered. "But Father has promised he will stay at our side as we pass into the next world, so that doesn't bother me that much anymore.

"The thing that really scares me is that we are going to forget. Like we just said, we forget *everything!* How can that be? How could we forget this place? But the forgetting is so complete, that once we are there, we don't want to come back. We fight to stay there, we fight to stay on the earth. It's like fighting to stay in prison. It doesn't make any sense, but we develop a terrible, loathsome fear of death, of coming back home. I don't know, but that strikes me as almost absurd. We get so involved in our earth-life that we fight to stay there! And we mourn those who proceed us to this side of the veil. That seems so incredibly . . . I don't know, but it's a little scary to me."

Elizabeth's eyes twinkled as she touched his arm. "Don't worry, I'll . . . " she started to tease.

"I know," he interrupted. *"I'll take care of you!"*

He had known her so long, he could almost read her mind. And he didn't want to leave her. He wanted to stay there forever with her, with the others. He wanted to stay there forever with his Parents and his Eldest Brother.

This place, all these people, it was enough for him. He was satisfied. He didn't need any more.

Young and tall, Luke was a man, but only barely—and in some ways he was still a child, for the growing process in the spirit took a very long time and maturity came slowly, with many lessons to learn. Still, he was supremely confident, for, unlike many others, he had felt the spark of perfection inside.

Luke's needs were simple. To him the world was already perfect. Every day, every hour was another chance to be happy, another chance for excitement or conversation with his friends. He embraced pessimism only when it came to his studies, for he wasn't fond of the classroom or the one-on-one time he had to spend with his teachers. He wasn't slow—in fact, quite the opposite, he was extremely bright—it was just that school could be so *boring!* So rigid, so stiff! Why did they have to study? All he heard was unending talk about the need to prepare. Was it really so important? Weren't there other things to do? What about the sun, and the beach, and the mountains, and the parks, his friends, and his dog, and his brothers. And there was flying! Oh, there was flying. How he dreamed of that day! Could there be anything in the universe that might be better than that? And there was his reading and his writing . . . and the list went on and on.

School. Well, yes, he knew that he had to learn, that he had to prepare, but sometimes he wondered. Was everything so urgent? Was it all so necessary?

A sudden smile crossed Luke's face as a powerful memory flooded his mind, a ridiculous recollection from a long, long time before.

* * *

He was young, foolishly young. Ammon was a little bit older, but still far too young to know better. On the warm summer days, he and Ammon used to lie on the grass and stare at the blue, dreaming of what it must be like to fly, effortlessly slipping among the stars and the sky, moving in space, zooming up, screaming down, calling from the mountaintops and landing on distant planets, feeling the coolness of the clouds on their lashes while laying their heads on great pillars of white, then falling through them like rain, but never touching the ground.

Yet, not being perfect like the Father, they were bound to the laws of their world. In the future, on the earth, some of them would learn to fly, but in the premortal existence there was no need. Still, like so many before them, they dreamed of that day when they would move like the Father in an effortless dance through the sky. It seemed to be inherent in some spirits, an internal, almost primordial yearning to fly.

So, working brother with brother, they came up with a plan. It was time for their world to see the first flying machine.

They spent hours studying the birds in the skies before they came up with their final design. Many happy hours were spent in construction, and when the contraption was finished, it certainly would have made the greatest scientist proud, though it was likely to bring a stab of fear to any aviator's heart. A wooden box and steel wings with various feathers glued on, it might have flown. But only for a moment. And only straight down.

About the time the child adventurers were dragging their contraption onto the roof for their maiden flight, their Father sought them out to see their flying machine. He stared at it proudly, a great smile on his face. He asked lots of questions as he admired their design. It was a beautiful contraption, he announced to his sons, and he was certain they had great futures in aero design. Still, it took him several minutes to convince them that it was probably not a good idea to launch their machine. "You'll scare all the birds," he explained with a smile. "But someday," he promised, "you will get your chance to fly."

* * *

Luke couldn't help but smile as he relived the memory. Ammon had been so certain, so convinced that their contraption would fly—so why, Luke had wondered as they were dragging it onto the roof, had he insisted that Luke be the first one to try? Upon hearing of Ammon's plan to launch his little brother into space, Father had laughed, then pulled Ammon aside to have a private chat. Ammon kicked the grass with his feet as his Father explained that Luke was his little brother and he had a responsibility to take care of him. Ammon had learned something that day about being a big brother. And Luke learned that his Father was patient with his children, even when they hatched foolish plans.

As Luke and Elizabeth sat in silence (for silence was a common and comfortable part of their world), his thoughts shifted to their older brother, Sam. Why had he left them, and without even a good-bye? Beth seemed to sense the change in his mood, for she turned to him with concern in her eyes. She started to speak when a small rabbit crawled slowly from under a nearby brush. She reached down to pick it up and held it carefully in her lap.

Luke watched Beth as she stroked the rabbit. She was so beautiful! Slender, with dark eyes and long, dark hair. And that smile! Oh, that smile, like a light from her soul! She was bubbly and quick, most called her lighthearted, or light-headed, some teased. What was the word Ammon used to describe her . . . giddy, yes, that was it. But she was also very smart, though she had to push herself to concentrate on the task at hand. It could take her hours to get dressed if she had the time, two hours to watch the sun rise, an hour to comb her hair. The problem was that there were just too many distractions, too many fascinating things to divert her. It could drive others crazy, but she didn't mind. Life was to savor, not to rush through!

Elizabeth stroked the rabbit gently, pulling lightly on its ears, then set it down to let it nibble on the grass at her feet.

Turning, she placed her hand on Luke's arm and looked him straight in the eye. "You're angry at Sam. I know that. But you've got to forgive him," she said, showing that she had indeed read his thoughts.

"I miss him," he said sadly, even angrily, as he stood suddenly and walked to the edge of the pool. "What was he thinking? I just don't understand! How could he do that . . . "

"He made his decision."

"That's not what I'm talking about. I can *understand* his decision. I can even accept it. So many people we know, people we have respected and loved, have chosen to support Lucifer. And who knows . . . " He stopped and his voice trailed off.

Beth's eyes clouded.

"What I don't understand," Luke continued, "and what makes me so angry, Beth, is how could Sam just pull up and leave, just take off like that without so much as saying good-bye? I mean, he knows, he understands how we all felt about him. He was our older brother, we loved him, and we love him still. He is one of my heroes, one of the sincerely good people in life, and yet he just slips away in the night. Tell me, Beth, does that seem like him?"

Luke's eyes were on fire from the betrayal and anger inside. Losing a brother, especially an older brother, and one he had idolized, was new and it was painful.

"He still loves you," Beth offered simply, cautiously. "You know that he does."

"No, Beth, I don't know that. At least not anymore."

"He did what he thought was right."

"If he did the right thing, he sure did it wrong. You don't just abandon the people you love. It's immature. Irresponsible. And it isn't like him."

"Sam is still a good person, Luke."

"Of course he's a good person! All of us are! But this thing, this conflict . . . it changes people. We've seen that already. It changes everything."

Luke ran his fingers through his hair as a dark pain crossed his face. He sighed wearily. He did not like these feelings, and he had no experience in how to deal with them.

Elizabeth watched him as he stood in silence by the side of the pool. She seemed to want to reach out and touch him, to offer comfort if she could, but Luke turned away as she moved to his side.

"You asked me if I'm scared," he whispered unhappily. "And I told you I wasn't, but that wasn't the truth. There is one thing that scares me. And it scares me to the core.

"I'm not afraid of failure. I'm not afraid for myself. I really believe that I will be all right. And so will you, Elizabeth. You are good. You are strong. You are one of the chosen. You will be called up and set apart. You will be saved for the end. There's no doubt in my mind. You will be held back for the great scene that will take place when we get to the last days of the earth.

"But I'm scared for the others. I worry for them, Sam and his friends. We can already see what the conflict has done to them. Sometimes I worry for Ammon. He can be so headstrong. And there are others, so many others! If they don't make it, and we lose them, we lose them forever! Forever, Beth! They will be separated forever, and that breaks my heart.

"So the concerns that I have do not rest in the plan. I have perfect faith in Jehovah. I know he will do what Father has asked him to do. He will not fail us, though some people think that he will. He will go. He will be perfect. I know he won't sin. And he loves us enough—even those who won't fight for him—he loves us enough to die for our sins.

"And I have faith in some of God's children. But not

everyone. Some of them have promised to help us, to stand at our side, but they are weak and might not even make it themselves."

Beth was silent for a while. Finally she spoke, picking her words carefully. "You're right, of course. Some are going to be lost, some of the people we love—maybe even Sam. And the battle is just getting under way. Still, Luke, there's hope, hope for everyone. The flaw isn't in the plan; it's in our own weakness. The plan offers such promise!" The joy of it shone in her eyes.

"What would you do, Luke?" she went on, biting her lip. "If you don't like what is happening, what would you propose?"

Luke clenched his jaw. "Lucifer may have his faults, I know that. He overreaches sometimes, and I certainly don't agree with everything he says. But his way, where *everyone* will come back—is that such a bad thing? How could it be heaven if we leave so many of our loved ones behind? Are Sam and the others so wrong? Our leaders say Lucifer's plan is evil, but sometimes I don't know."

Beth stepped back, her forehead wrinkled with worry. "Not everyone who has joined Lucifer did it for the reasons that you said," she answered. "Many of them want power. That's the only thing they care about. And some of them hate Jehovah. You can hear it when they talk; you can see it in their eyes. They don't care about helping others. They aren't like you or me. They want to defeat him, bring him down, cause him pain. So let's not be overgenerous when we discuss Lucifer's schemes. People follow him for many reasons, and most of them aren't pure."

"Do you put Sam in that category?" Luke quickly replied. "He is our brother. Is he evil too?"

Elizabeth shook her head. "I don't know," she said sadly.

"That remains to be seen. But listen to me, Luke. I want you to think, think back on the Council when Father presented the plan. All of us were there, each and every one. We all had a chance to learn of the plan. But after the Council, when we were on our way home, do you remember what you told me? Do you remember what you said? Think of that, Luke, for I think it might be the key."

Luke nodded slowly. "I remember," he said.

"What did you say, Luke? What did you notice about the spirits who gathered to hear of the plan?"

"I said that everyone was there. But not everyone was listening."

"Yes, Luke! That's right! Everyone was there, but some people wouldn't listen. And if they don't listen, if they don't follow the plan, then we can't help them, Luke. They have to listen, make a decision, and eventually choose their course, for that's *the* central part of the plan. We can't choose for them—not you, not me, not even Jehovah or Father can. God can't force his children to become like him. It's something they have to want, a blessing they have to fight for and be willing to sacrifice to attain. And if they choose to follow Satan, to surrender their will, if they choose the ugliness of a path that offers no agency, then God cannot stop them, for they are free to choose."

Luke nodded slowly. He knew that was true. But he had so many doubts. And it pained him too much to push his feelings aside. He looked up at the sky, searching for the sun through the trees, then nodded his head toward the path. "We ought to be getting back," he said.

Elizabeth didn't move, though she followed his eyes. "Luke," she said gently, her eyes softer now. "Listen! This is important! I'm just like you. I have my own fears and doubts. I think everyone does. I used to be scared of the pain—the pain of birth and living in a physical world, the pain of hunger and sickness, of death or abuse, of loneliness or neglect, of all of the things that we must experience to learn. And I used to be scared . . . no, I used to be terrified of being a mother. I mean, family is the whole purpose. That's what this whole thing is about, and I used to be terrified that I might fail, or that one of my children might die early, or that . . . " she glanced quickly away, then continued slowly, " . . . or that one of my children wouldn't love me. We've seen how that feels.

"But I think I am beginning to understand these things and how they fit with the plan. I think I can see the big picture and how faith makes anything possible. And now the only thing I'm afraid of is that when it's over, when it's all said and done, when I have been to the mortal world and my earth-life is through, when I come back to the Father and sit at the feet of the Savior, I'm afraid that I won't be able to look Him in the eye, that I won't have earned the right to come back to Him. That is my greatest fear now, that I won't be worthy to come home."

Luke held her by the shoulders and looked into her eyes. "You will be worthy," he whispered. "I know your heart. You will eventually be like Father. You will be perfect one day."

Beth trembled lightly as she put a hand to her lips. "I hope so," she whispered with awful uncertainty. She was silent a moment as she stared off through the trees.

"We ought to go," Luke said. "Ammon will be leaving for the rally, and I want to talk to him before he goes."

Elizabeth grabbed another strand of hair and twirled it nervously. "I don't think he should go," she said. "It isn't right. And I think it is dangerous for him to go there alone."

"Maybe. But he insists. I've tried to argue, but he won't change his mind." Luke stood up and moved for the trail.

"Come on," he said. "Let's make sure we see him before he goes."

"Luke," she said hesitantly, "before we go, there's something that I need to tell you."

"What is it?" he asked quickly, knowing she had something important to say.

She took a step back, and her face brightened visibly. "I talked with Father this morning. We spent a long time together. It was so wonderful."

Luke nodded and waited. "And . . . did he . . . ?"

"Yes. He told me my mission, Luke. He told me where I fit in the plan. And it is so . . . " she shivered, and a sudden tear wet her eye. "It is so incredible, Luke! You won't even believe. I'm so excited. But I'm scared! In fact, I'm terrified. It is nothing I had dreamed of, not in a million years." She reached for his hand. "I want to tell you, Luke. I want to share everything. But He said I couldn't tell anyone, at least not yet."

chapter seven

Far to the east, away from the valiant children of God, along a wide and tree-covered trail, a group of Lucifer's followers were walking up the side of a steep hill. The small group of men and women had been tasked to dig out a clearing on the crest of the foothill that had been identified as an ideal location for one of the many housing projects that seemed to be sprouting up everywhere. People were flooding into Lucifer's cities, most of them recent converts to his plan, and his followers were in desperate need of dwellings to house the newcomers.

It was a bright day, but a constant overcast seemed to hang over the mountains that surrounded Lucifer's expanding city, a mix of dust from hasty construction and soot from the fires of industry that burned constantly. The overcast didn't block out the light entirely, however, and the shadows under the trees flickered gloomily as the branches moved with the wind. Most of the group was silent as they marched, focused as always on the task at hand.

Samuel, the oldest of the men, lagged behind the main body of the group. A young woman walked just ahead of him. She was slightly older than he was and, like all of God's children, extremely beautiful. Because she was a newcomer, the strain of living among Lucifer's followers had not entirely sucked the glow from her face. Her escort—all newcomers were assigned someone to assist them in the transition—walked ten feet ahead, talking solemnly with another woman, an old friend.

Sam watched the newcomer out of the corner of his eye, then picked up his pace until he reached her side. She glanced over and smiled, a hollow grin with no warmth. "How are you?" Samuel asked as he fell into step next to her.

"Fine," she answered blankly.

"It's going to be a busy day." He nodded up the trail. "We've got a lot of work to do."

"I don't mind hard work. I spend all of my time inside, cooped in a cramped corner, and I'm looking forward to being outdoors."

"Have you been here very long?"

The woman glanced around quickly. "Not too long, I guess."

"You like it here?"

"Of course," she answered quickly. A little too quickly, Sam thought. She glanced sideways toward him. "How about you?" she asked.

Samuel squished his face. "I haven't been here that long. But at least I don't need an escort." He nodded ahead.

"No, I don't mean how long have you been here. I mean do you like it? Are things working out for you?"

"Absolutely . . . usually. I suppose."

They walked in silence a while. The trail became steeper. The trees began to thin out, and the shadows weakened along their path. Patches of gray and brown sky came into view through the trees. The group had spread out along the trail as they neared their destination, where the real work would begin. Reaching the top, the young people paused to regroup and rest, laying out on the grassy patches to absorb the sun. Samuel came to a stop over a fresh patch of loam. He bent at the knees and took a handful of rich mountain soil, pressing it in his hands, then letting the black earth sift through his fingers. It was soft and mulchy, so rich and full of nutrients it almost balled in his hand.

"Look at this!" he exclaimed quietly, momentarily forgetting the woman. "I could grow *anything* in this soil. I could make this hilltop blossom with a garden that would bring tears to your eyes."

The young woman listened, then bent down beside him. "I don't think this spot will ever host a garden. It will be buildings and roads."

Sam nodded, then pushed himself up. "But we need gardens, too. And if they would let me . . . " His voice trailed off, then became resolute, his eyes narrow and focused, his jaw set tight. "Yes, . . . of course. That's his decision. So be it then!"

The woman looked at his dirty hands, then stood and turned to look out over the bustling valley below the ridge. The shadows were long and the new buildings were dark and tall, some shining with glass, others dully reflecting the light from their dark rock and cement façades. Turning away, she glanced again at Sam. He was staring at her. "Where did you come from?" he asked.

"Oh, you know," she waved absently to the west.

Sam nodded. "Did you come here alone?"

"No. I came with a friend and one of my sisters. But they didn't stay long." She was silent for a minute, then added, "I haven't heard from them since they left."

Sam pressed his lips together and nodded. How many

times had he heard the same thing before? She wiped a dusty hand across her face as they stood side by side.

"Can I ask you something?" he said.

"I guess so," she replied.

"Do you believe *everything* that you hear over here?"

She thought a long moment. "I'm close to understanding, I think."

"So it's all fitting together?"

She looked at him suspiciously. "Yeah, I guess so," she answered cautiously.

"You know, some people who choose to follow Lucifer begin to have second thoughts. I don't know, I've seen lots of reasons, but the bottom line, sometimes people just change their minds. If you think that might be happening, then I think we should talk. There are some things I could tell you that will help you, I think."

The woman didn't answer, and Sam glanced toward her, noting the hidden look of uncertainty in her eye. She kept her head low, and Samuel studied her as they began to walk again.

He was going to have to watch her carefully. If she showed even one more sign of unbelief, he would pull her aside and have a talk.

He lowered his voice and leaned toward her. "You can trust me," he confided, trying to gain her confidence. "I am your friend." He patted her shoulder. "We'll talk later."

chapter eight

Flags. Thousands of them, perhaps ten thousand or more.

They waved from every pillar and column at the top of the ring; beautiful multicolored flags of black and dark green, silky and light, they fluttered in the wind, banners of power, a great call to arms. Each flag held a crescent moon over a short stubby cross, the emblem of the new party, the loyal opposition, those who were on the rise. Five enormous banners, two hundred feet square, each with the same green crescent and black cross, moved in the gentle wind from tall poles that had been erected around the huge outdoor park. The banners rippled lightly but didn't spread out, for the wind wasn't strong enough to unfurl them yet. But to the west, storm clouds were rising and soon would be there.

A gently sloping bowl of green grass rose in every direction, with the stage in the center and the bottom of the bowl. Ancient stone columns and arches lined the top of the park. The crowd gathered in a full circle around the huge stage, which rose some fifty feet in the air. They gathered in groups as families and friends. There were children among them, but only a few, which was unusual, for normally there were many children around. Some of the participants came alone, but many brought others with them, for all were encouraged to help spread the word. Nobody knew how many people had gathered that day. It was impossible to count them; they numbered as the sands of the sea. Most of the afternoon rally had been spent with other, less well-known speakers, a few musical numbers, and a youth choir, but it was barely a warm-up, for everyone knew why the people were there.

The sun was just setting, casting long shadows eastward, when, amid a frenzy of screaming and clapping and a full-throated band—a band that played a new music, sounds that had never been heard and with a drumbeat that was odd and exciting to the crowd—the great leader finally emerged on the stage. The crowd went wild, clapping and screaming and stamping their feet. He stood and lifted his face to his followers, encouraging them as he cupped his hands to his ears, lifting his arms in a gesture of more. The crowd went wild again and a great wind suddenly blew, lifting the banners around them, flapping the light silk like another drum in the wind. The huge banners spread out, casting long shadows that flickered in the wind. Lucifer noted and pointed to the banners, as if he were surprised. The banners billowed and waved against the sky, almost blocking the sun. The crowd fell silent, in awe, then quickly whipped themselves into a frenzy again.

It must be an omen! They screamed in delight.

The wind grew more gusty as storm clouds drew near. The people roared in approval as Lucifer moved across the stage, then lifted his arms, asking for silence. The crowd howled even louder. They simply could not hold back. Thunder rolled in the distance, promising rain, the dark clouds gusting forward on the sudden, cold wind. The crowd seemed not to notice as they clapped and screamed. They had waited for this day for a very long time.

Finally, many minutes later, they fell into silence, their pent-up emotion giving way to exhaustion. Lucifer watched them and waited, then spread his arms and smiled.

They were his power. They were all he had. He was nothing without them.

But they were enough.

And as long as they were willing to follow, as long as they were willing to cry and scream and pledge their undying support, as long as they were willing to believe him, even knowing in their hearts, somewhere deep in their souls, that he was lying to them, as long as they were willing to listen, and follow, and do what he said, then he would grow strong, drawing more power from them. As long as they were with him, standing loyally at his side, then nothing could stop him. His success was assured.

And they were willing to follow, that was the bottom line. No one had forced them to be here! They had chosen to come. Without them, he was nothing but a silver-tongued devil with great hair and white teeth. But with them—oh, with them! There was nothing he couldn't do.

As Lucifer looked out upon them, his followers, his servants, those who brought him such power, he shivered with excitement. He couldn't help smile.

* * *

Ammon stood alone near the stone arches that defined the top of the park, right next to the raging flags and huge banners that beat themselves in the wind. He watched both the speaker and the crowd as the assembly wore on, sometimes astonished, sometimes afraid. It was like watching some magic, something he could not understand, the way Lucifer manipulated their emotions, like they were an empty bag, waiting for him to fill them with whatever he desired—hate, anger, jealousy, fear, lust, ambition, or irrational rage. They were pliable, like soft putty, wanting to be molded by his hand. And it was clear, as he watched, that these people had surrendered their will.

The wind blew clouds of dust before the rising storm, and Ammon pulled his sash over his face. The crowd did not notice the gusting wind, their enthusiasm unabated as the speaker went on. Ammon began to move among the people, searching the faces in the crowd.

His brother was here, somewhere in this mass of people.

Lucifer held up his arms, and the mob fell silent, an enormous sea of people waiting to hang on his every word. He moved center stage and turned in a slow circle, seeming to acknowledge each individual in the crowd. The people took a breath and held it, almost breathing as one. The sky grew dark from the clouds that had blown in from the west, casting dim shadows in an almost purple-blue light. Lightning flashed in the distance, illuminating his face. He spoke, his voice a rumble that echoed over the crowd.

"My brothers and sisters," he cried. "Thank you! Thank you for coming! Your participation, your support, your enthusiasm and passion, everything you offer—it means so much to me. This incredible—" he stopped and turned in a circle again, his voice almost cracking with emotion and pride. "This incredible crowd of great people! It is more than I could ask for! You are all that I'll ever need!"

The crowd cried and stamped their feet, going crazy again, cheering and screaming and clapping their hands. The flags rippled in the wind and the band struck up a new song, the drums beating wildly, the crowd joining in the rhythm as they waved their hands in the air.

Lucifer watched carefully. There was so much energy! So much passion and heat! He lifted his head, holding his face to the sky, and slowly closed his eyes as the adulation washed over him like crashing waves of warm sound. Time seemed to pass slowly. He opened his eyes and lowered his head. "Brothers and sisters," he continued in his low, rolling voice, "each of you has come here for the same reason. After a great debate, after a great contest of ideas, each of you, each of us, have come to believe the same thing. We have discussed this before; there is nothing new I can say. We have debated it so long now it is beginning to wear on my nerves.

"But let me say once again, because I want you to know. I don't mean to speak ill of our brother. I know that you love him, and I love him too! He has done so much for me, taught me so many things. But this scheme . . . this risky, dangerous, salvation scheme! It is going to destroy us! It will destroy *most* of you!

"And so I ask you to consider, consider one final time. Is that what you want? Do you want to fight for salvation? Do you want to fight tooth and nail, to claw your way through some earth-life of pain and gut-wrenching sorrow, do you want to crawl like a maggot through the drivel and slop, just to fight your way *back to where you are now?* Are you willing to do that? And for what purpose, I ask. How many will He lose? How many of you and your loved ones will not make it back?

"It is a terrible cruelty, a selfish and sadistic plan, to ask you to go through that just so *they* get more power!" Lucifer stabbed with his finger at some unseen enemy that the crowd hated now. "Why must you suffer? Is that what we really want? Is it love that demands such a high price of you? Or is it love that *I* offer? Is there more love in *my* way?"

The crowd screamed with emotion, a wild craze in their

eyes. Yes! Yes! It had to be true. He was the one who loved them, not Elohim and Jehovah. The Father didn't love them; he had a selfish, cruel plan!

But Lucifer would save them! Oh, and they loved him so. He would save them from the suffering. He would save every one!

So they cried and they shouted, and they embraced his offer anew.

And the banners waved behind him, lifting in the great wind, casting dark, lonely shadows across the great crowd.

The rally went on until dusk, Lucifer gauging the crowd, sensitive to the fact that he could keep them going only so long. He sensed their waning energy about the same time it began to drizzle, the precursor to the heavy rains that were just a few miles away. He closed suddenly with a wave of his arms, a final promise of victory, and a cry of encouragement, then moved in a circle, seeming to look everyone in the eye. With a wave of farewell, he marched from the stage.

A lieutenant was waiting at the base of the platform. He wrapped the great leader in a banner, draping it over his shoulders, and led him away, down a long tunnel that would take them away from the crowd. A large entourage, all of them men, followed the great leader as he walked down the dark tunnel, his closest advisors crowding near, all of them congratulating him with exaggerated praise. As the group of men entered the tunnel, the storm clouds broke loose, sending cold shafts of rain driven before a harsh wind. The master looked back and laughed, knowing his people would be utterly drenched.

In the background, against the tunnel wall, a stocky man stood in the shadows. Balaam wiped a hand across his stubbled face as his master walked by. Then he turned to his young friend and smiled pleasantly.

"Was that so bad?" he offered. "Can you see now that the evil rumors you hear about us are nothing but exaggerations and lies?"

Luke stood in the shadows and followed Lucifer with his eyes, watching as he passed and walked down the dim hall. The soft light caught the great leader's hair and cast a strong shadow over his face. He towered above his followers, so strong and tall. And yes, there were times . . . there were times when he seemed to speak the truth. But there were other times, other words, when he seemed so angry and bitter! What were his motives? What did he really want? Was he in this for his people or only himself? Luke had to wonder, and he felt a sinking feeling inside.

Balaam watched him closely, measuring the look in his eyes. "Would you like to meet him?" he asked excitedly.

Luke shook his head. "I've seen enough," he quickly replied.

"If you would like, I could arrange a time when you could . . ."

"No, thank you, Balaam, I've seen enough."

"What if we were to . . . ?"

"No, Master Balaam, I just want time to think. But thank you for inviting me. I appreciate your effort and time." Luke touched Balaam on the shoulder, then moved to walk up the tunnel, toward the crowd and the rain. Turning, he lowered his voice. "This is our secret," he reminded. "That was part of the agreement. You wouldn't talk to Ammon if I agreed to come."

"Yes, yes, of course. You know I won't betray you. You can always trust me, Luke."

Luke nodded appreciatively. "Thank you," he said as he turned away.

"I will be thinking of you, Luke," Balaam called after him. "Be careful. And think about what I told you today."

Luke waved over his shoulder but didn't stop or look back. He walked toward the shadows of the night sky and exited the tunnel, stepping into the rain.

Balaam watched him go, then turned to follow Lucifer's noisy crowd. Though he was one of those servants who had chosen to follow Lucifer, he stayed far behind, for he was not a member of the inner circle—that much was clear.

Lucifer walked at the head of the group of men, moving with long strides and renewed energy. He could have gone on for hours if the crowd had let him. He was high on the emotion he had sapped from his followers, the experience leaving them exhausted but making him come alive. How he held them, how he cowed them, how he sapped their energy dry! And he loved it. He needed it. And he wanted more. He would never be satisfied. He was addicted to them now.

As he walked down the tunnel, the sound of the crowd drifted behind him and Lucifer slowed and looked back, glancing over his shoulder. He wanted to go back and climb onto the stage. He wanted to stand before them and lather them into a frenzy again. He wanted to hear them and see the wild look in their eyes. His chest constricted suddenly. How he thrilled at the crowd!

* * *

The rain poured like a waterfall from the sky, blown by the wind into sheets of cold, biting water. The crowd began to run as the thunder and lightning beat on the ground. The people scattered in all directions, most of them holding jackets or blankets over their heads. The wind blew the rain, forming a wall of cold water that soaked Ammon completely as he walked through the running crowd.

"Sam!" he cried above the howl of the wind.

The crowd ignored him. He called his brother again. No one stopped to offer assistance, though, in the darkness, behind a window, someone was watching him.

* * *

The tunnel began to ascend and the group walked through a large set of double doors into a small room. There, Lucifer's mood suddenly soured. He turned to his lieutenants. "Did you see them?" he demanded.

A moment of silence followed. "Who?" one of his lieutenants replied carefully.

"Traitors. They were out there. The Father has sent out his spies!"

No one seemed to know quite what to think, and they were slow to respond. A hush fell over the room as Lucifer stared at his men. "You didn't see them?" he demanded. "How could you be so blind?" Again, no one answered.

Lucifer searched the faces of his men, then pointed to a man at the back of the room. "Come here," he commanded, with a twitch of his finger.

Balaam came forward and bowed, his lips trembling, his eyes wide in awe.

"Will you do something for me?" Lucifer asked as he placed his hand on Balaam's shoulder.

Balaam nodded eagerly.

"Will you lie for me?" Lucifer asked him.

"Sir, I already have."

"Would you give up anything?"

"You know that I will."

Lucifer smiled, then bent over and whispered in Balaam's ear.

chapter nine

Ammon left the park, which was now empty, and walked the long, deserted streets. It was dark now, and the pavement, wide and beautifully inlaid with precious metal and fine stones, rolled with high water from the sudden downpour, the rainwater running like a small river along the edge of the street. Overhead, the clouds remained dark and roiling, though the rain had slowed to a drizzle, hardly more than a mist in the air. Lightning flashed in the distance, way beyond in the east, too far away for the sound of the thunder to carry, but close enough to flicker in the night. Somewhere in the heavens the moon hung in the night, bright and white and so close it covered nearly a fourth of the sky, but it was blotted out behind the thick bank of clouds.

Ammon walked slowly and stared at his feet.

Everything was different. The city had changed.

He had not been there for a long time, not since he was a child, but he could see that the buildings were taller and much closer together. Every available space had been crammed with a structure of some kind, most of them plain and quickly built, the craftsmanship shoddy, the architecture haphazard and of ignoble design. He noted the holes in the pavement and spreading cracks in the road. And there were other signs that the city was not what it used to be: a smell in the air he did not recognize, whispering voices, and bright neon lights, books in the storefronts he had not seen before, more people crammed into fewer buildings, but less activity on the streets, the faces less friendly, less open and content. A great shadow held the city. He could sense it. He could see it. He could feel it in the air. Approaching the corner, Ammon glanced to his right. A grassy park lay at the end of the block, the grass trampled into dirt by a hundred thousand stomping feet. Another park, another rally, another patch of dead grass. He glanced around him, looking for people. There were a couple of men down the street and a small woman on the corner, but other than that he was completely alone.

Ahead of him a young man stepped quickly out of a tall building, pushing back the heavy glass door and emerging into the night. He stood for a moment, glancing in both directions, then walked toward Ammon, a vacant and indifferent look in his eye. Passing by, the stranger whispered, "You don't belong here."

Ammon turned quickly. "What did you say?"

The stranger didn't slow or look back, but walked on in silence, his shawl drawn around him, his shoulders hunched, his head down, his eyes on his feet.

"I don't belong here!" Ammon repeated.

But neither did Sam. And yet here they were.

All Ammon wanted was to see Sam, to talk with him, even if just for a short time. He hadn't come to drag him back. He couldn't do that, for Sam, like everyone, had his moral agency. But Ammon needed to see him, to ask him, "Why? Why did you choose this? What opportunity have you found? What does this bring you? Don't you miss your family?"

Ammon knew that none of Sam's friends, not a single one, had chosen to follow Jehovah. And yet all of them at one time had been good, in some ways exceptional men—worthy, honorable, believing, and kind. But they had all made the wrong decision, and Ammon couldn't understand why. And he couldn't just accept it and go on with his life. He had to try to understand them or he would never find peace.

Ammon walked toward an intersection and came to a stop. He stood there a moment, wondering which way he should go.

* * *

Sam had always been a bit of a rebel, one of those who needed to push against the crowd. If others said walk, he would run; when they said stop, he would go; when his teachers explained the class rules, he would always ask why. From the time he was young, he was independent and free, the type of person all the other youth wanted to be around and the older folks admired for his talents and smile. A natural leader, he moved comfortably among a diverse circle of friends while remaining one step aloof, always keeping a part of his life to himself. He was extremely good-looking, lean, lanky, a bit of a curl in his hair, which he wore back in a small wave at the front of his head. And though he was clearly his own man and not one to be pulled by the crowd, he was also fiercely loyal to his family, and as protective of his younger brothers and sisters as any older brother could be.

Looking at it now, Ammon recognized the irony in the path Sam had chosen to walk, a path that was certain to relieve him of his agency, to reduce him to a slave, no longer unique, no longer able to choose, no freedom, no expression or thought, a slave to his master, only doing his will. For such a free spirit, it would prove a bitter hell.

Sam was enough older than Ammon that by the time Ammon could remember, Sam was in and out of the house, sometimes living on his own, sometimes with his family, sometimes with his friends. Ammon's earliest memory of his older brother was one afternoon when Sam came home from the university to visit during a summer break. Ammon remembered very clearly Sam racing into the huge summer home, accompanied by some friends, all of them excited and laughing, anxious to have some fun and relax. At a time when most people wore robes tied with multicolored sashes, or simple pantsuits that snapped in the front, Sam had taken to wearing white pullover shirts and long trousers with overcoats that reached to his knees. Ammon watched in amazement as he burst into the room, his dark hair curled back in that incredible wave, his teeth flashing constantly in a bright, friendly smile. Sam was so much larger than life, Ammon was almost afraid of him. He was such a powerful presence, so handsome and confident, smiling and laughing, his eyes sparkling and alive.

As Sam moved through the room, slapping shoulders, planting kisses, embracing his family and friends, Ammon pulled back, pressing against the nearest wall, wishing he could turn and run and hide down the hall. Then Sam saw his little brother and the bewildered look on his face and he stopped suddenly, holding up both of his hands. "Wait!" Sam exclaimed. "Who is this handsome lad? Could this be my baby brother? No! He's too big. And look at those eyes! What an incredible face. Look at this angel. He is even more perfect than I remember!" Sam broke into a smile that seemed as bright as the sun. He took a step forward, but Ammon stepped back. Sam was simply too tall, too strong, and too beautiful.

Sam's face softened as he studied the expression in his

little brother's eyes; then he fell to his knees, lowering himself to Ammon's level, and slowly, almost tenderly, extended his arms. "Ammon, don't you know me? I am your older brother," he said. "I know I've been away a long time, and you have forgotten. But while you may not know me, I know all about you. I have watched you and loved you since the day you were born. And I have missed you so much. You are one of the reasons I had to come home. I had to see you, to measure you, to see how you've grown. So, please, don't be frightened. I promise you, brother, I am your very best friend."

Sam kept his arm extended and cocked his head to one side, staring tenderly into Ammon's eyes. He extended his fingers, then beckoned to him. "I have missed you so much, Ammon. Won't you be my friend?"

And with that, it was over. Ammon ran into his arms. Even now, as an adult, he remembered the feeling of comfort and love. Sam held him tight, as they rocked back and forth in the hall. Then Sam lifted him quickly and tossed him in the air. Ammon squealed with delight and held his hands to his eyes. "Come on," Sam whispered in Ammon's ear. "Let's get out of here. I understand you and Luke have been busy building a flying machine. This is so great! Will you show it to me? Then let's go for a walk, just you and me. I want to hear about your friends. I want to hear everything."

The two brothers spent most of Sam's vacation together, reading, talking, listening to music, and playing games. They spent a lot of time in the garden, for Sam loved it there. He had a genuine touch, an almost uncanny ability to make things blossom and grow. Ammon came to believe Sam could *feel* the plants and flowers, that somehow he could sense what they needed in order to thrive.

Sam also had a wonderful voice, soft and tender, like a

whisper in the night, and he sang to Ammon in the darkness, tender songs of loved ones and robins and strawberry leaves, his sweet voice so quiet it was barely heard in the dark. Sometimes they would talk through the night. Sam knew so many things about people and places that were far, far away.

The days passed quickly. It seemed to Ammon that it was only one long summer afternoon, but the time soon came for Sam to go back to school. Once again, Sam bent down to look his baby brother in the eye and held out his arms, asking for one more embrace. "I'll be back," he promised. "I love you. We are brothers. That will always be true."

Several days later, Ammon's mother had found him hiding under the bushes in the enormous backyard, wailing in agony, his cheeks stained with huge, rolling tears. She picked him up and held him, brushing the tears from his eyes. "What's the matter, Ammon?" she asked tenderly.

Ammon buried his head in her shoulder. "I can't tell you," he cried.

"Of course you can, baby. Now tell me, what's wrong."

Ammon pulled back and shamefully wiped the tears from his eyes. "Go ahead," his mother prodded in her comforting way.

Ammon buried his head on her shoulder again. "I just miss Sam so much!" he cried through his heartbroken tears.

* * *

As Ammon stood in the drizzle and looked down the long, empty street, as he felt the cold chill and wet mist on his face, as he stood in the darkness in a city he no longer recognized, the tall buildings around him and the rain on his cheek, he realized that he missed his older brother as much as he had ever missed anything in his life.

Is this what earth-life will be like? he wondered to himself.

Somewhere deep inside, will I miss my home then like I miss my big brother now?

* * *

Ammon heard the sound of footsteps and turned to see a group of men walking toward him. They came from far down the street, down near the park, which was now a wet, muddy mess. Marching toward him, they stayed close together and held their heads low. There were five, maybe six, and none of them spoke as they walked. An older woman followed them closely, wearing a dark, flowing robe, holding one corner of the garment to keep the hem off the wet street. The group approached him in silence and formed a small circle, four or five feet away.

"Hello," Ammon greeted them.

None of the young men replied.

Ammon turned quickly to look into each of their faces. The strangers watched him closely, their eyes cold and intense. He felt a sudden shiver of something he had not felt before. The woman pushed through the circle with a large and powerful arm, her face tightly puckered, her lips pressed into a cruel frown.

"What do you want here?" she asked before she even came to a stop.

Ammon paused. "I have business," he answered.

"You have no business here. We know our own kind."

Ammon shot a quick glance at the men and felt another shiver run down his spine. He turned back to face her, his shoulders defiant and square. He took a step toward her, but the woman did not step back. The circle tightened up with a shuffle of feet.

"What do you want?" she demanded again.

"I'm looking for my brother," Ammon replied.

The woman snorted, an exaggerated look of surprise on her face. "Oh, he's looking for *his brother,*" she cried sarcastically. "But we're all brothers, boy, isn't that what all you guys teach? Or don't you believe Him? Have you too turned away?" She laughed to her men, then thumped him once on the chest. Ammon recoiled at her finger. No one had ever touched him in anger before! And it offended him. It stirred him unlike anything he had ever felt before.

Ammon stepped back. "Do you know my brother Sam?" he demanded. "If you do, I'd like to see him. If not, I'll be on my way."

The woman turned and pointed with her hand down the street. "I don't know your brother," she grunted. "And neither do you. And now you should go. You have no business here."

Ammon hesitated, then pushed through the circle, holding her glaring eyes as he passed. As he moved by her, she leaned into him, her anger burning inside her, a yellow fire in her eyes. It smoldered so powerfully he could almost smell it on her breath; like a wet, musky smoke, she smelled of loathing and hate.

"See you later, *boy,*" she sneered as he passed. He didn't answer, but turned his back to her and walked again, all alone, down the dark, empty street.

Three blocks later, he heard another set of footsteps behind him. Slowing, he heard a voice that he recognized.

Master Balaam, the great teacher, one of his most trusted friends, one of the most respected instructors and mentors at the university, stepped from the shadows and into the light. Ammon turned quickly, a look of relief on his face. "Balaam!" he shouted. Then he took a step back, for Balaam looked different, and it startled him. His face was thin and dark, his eyes sullen and mean, his jawbone protruding over a long and sinewy neck. Ammon watched him a moment, then stepped toward him again.

Balaam stood his ground. "You shouldn't be here, Ammon," he said in a gravely voice. "We just want to be left alone. Sam—all the others. We don't need your interference. We are satisfied."

Ammon stopped suddenly. "You have talked to Sam?" he asked urgently.

"Of course I have, Ammon. I talk to him every day."

"I need to see him, Master Balaam."

"Why?" Balaam snorted. "So you can try and convert him. Don't you people ever give up? Like I told you before, we are satisfied. We don't need anything. All we ask of your people is that you leave us alone."

Ammon took another step forward. "Sam is my brother, Balaam, and you know how I feel. Won't you take me to him? I know he would talk to me."

Balaam shook his head. "He doesn't want to see you, Ammon, he told me himself. He said I should tell you that it was time to give up. He wants you to leave here and never come back."

Ammon shook his head bitterly. "I don't believe you," he said.

Balaam knew that he wouldn't. The young could be so naïve, so idealistic, as if people couldn't disappoint or change. "You know, Ammon, you had your chance," he said. "You and Sam could be working together. I made you an offer that night on the mountain, but you chose another way."

Ammon gestured around him. "From what I've seen, there isn't anything here that I want to be part of."

"Don't you want to be a part of Sam? Don't you want to have him in your life?"

Ammon answered slowly. "You know I love Sam. And he

knows that too. But Jehovah is my Savior, and he is the one I will serve."

"Hmmm," Balaam wondered, pretending to think to himself. "Then let me ask you something, Ammon. I notice that Michael the Archangel is forming his army. He has chosen his leaders from the good and the strong, and put them in charge of his messengers, valiant groups of women and men. And I noticed, Ammon, that when he selected his leaders, he did not choose you. What's the matter, Ammon, aren't you smart enough? Or good enough? Or is it that you aren't one of his boys, you know, one of the group who always get recognized?"

Ammon was slow to answer, and Master Balaam smiled. "So, you *have* thought about it. And why shouldn't you? If I were you, I'd be angry. Doesn't he care about you?"

Ammon shook his head. "Won't you take me to Sam? That's all I came here for."

Balaam switched his voice. It was intense, almost angry, and bitter as brown water from a dead well. "Now you listen to me, Ammon," he said in a sneer. "I asked you to join us, but you rejected me. I will ask once more, but this is the last chance you will get. Come! Join with us. Work with Sam and me. Lucifer will make you a leader over ten thousand strong. He will make you a commander of others. You will be recognized. Michael may ignore you, but we see your strength. We know your talents and what lies ahead. What a future you will have, if you come join with me. You and your brother, commanding together, rallying other soldiers for the salvation of men. And I'm talking *all* men, Ammon, both the weak and the strong, not just those who are fortunate enough to be chosen by God. Remember, my dear Ammon, you were not chosen before. Will you be selected to be saved by your unforgiving God, he whom you claim to be perfect, but whom I wonder about?"

Ammon's chest tightened in anger. He would do it right now; he would stand up and fight. Balaam saw his face tighten, and he took a step forward. "He won't do it," he whispered. "You believe in Him; I know that. But deep down inside, I think you wonder too. Will Jehovah go down and be perfect? Not even one tiny sin? Think about that, Ammon. Is it possible? He will be spit upon and reviled, mocked and hated by far lesser men, and yet he will never, not once, have an uncharitable thought, not a single pang of regret or ounce of self-pity. He will be hated and beaten, like some mongrel dog, while lesser men pass their judgment—and you believe he will *never, not once,* feel any anger or wish for revenge? Remember, it won't be good enough that he do the right thing. He can't even *feel* the wrong way, for that too is a sin. He must have perfect control over his body, his will, and his mind. He can't experience a moment of selfish anger or miss a single opportunity to serve. He can't entertain one self-serving notion, unkind thought, or harsh word! Not even *one* sin! Who can do that, I ask? It is impossible.

"So ask yourself, Ammon. Will he go down and be perfect. Or will he spoil the plan? It is foolishness, and you know it is."

The great teacher moved forward, glaring into Ammon's face. "Look at me, Ammon," he sneered in disgust. "Look at me, Ammon; look into my eyes. Do you see hope and salvation? Is this the face of the damned?"

Ammon lowered his head as his heart slammed in his chest. But he swallowed and turned, forcing the anger down. He refused to get caught up in an argument with Balaam, for he had heard everything, heard all of their arguments before. "Will you take me to Sam?" he asked a final time.

"Don't you see?" Balaam sneered, his lips curling into a dark scowl. "Sam's not your brother. He doesn't care about you anymore. He wants you to join him; but if you don't, that is fine. In that case, he has pledged to fight you. Now go, Ammon, go! But keep this in mind. We have one of your brothers, and we are coming for the other one. And we are not through with you."

Balaam snorted and Ammon turned away. Walking down the street, he felt a cold stare, the dark piercing eyes boring into the back of his head.

* * *

Sam watched the exchange from a dark window that looked out over the street. He leaned against the glass, a lonely look on his face. Inside he was torn, almost twisted in two. A part of him, a hungry part buried deep in his soul, wanted to run to his brother, fall on his shoulders, and cry with relief.

He wanted to go home. He had been gone too long.

But he knew that he couldn't. There was no way he could now.

He felt a heart-wrenching shudder as his brother walked away. And as he leaned against the window, watching Ammon walk down the long, lonely street, the blackness inside him seemed to only grow worse, the isolation more bitter and the frustration more sharp.

He swallowed and turned, jamming his fists in his eyes.

How he longed for the comfort and feel of his land. How he longed for his family. How he wished he could go home!

chapter ten

The sun was just coming up when Ammon walked through the front door. The first thing he noted was the silence. Normally there would have been some kind of music—Beth would have made certain of that, even if it were merely her singing to get the day under way. But not this morning. She was quiet, and there was no music there. The enormous house seemed lonely and deserted, its huge rooms and open balconies begging for the voices of friends.

Elizabeth was waiting, her face drawn in worry, her cheeks moist and soft beneath her red eyes. Luke was resting on the couch, but he bolted upright at the first sound of Ammon's footsteps. Beth rushed toward Ammon, with Luke only a half step behind.

"Did you see him?" Luke asked as he moved to Ammon's side. Ammon looked at him wearily and barely moved his head to the side.

"Nothing?" Luke demanded. Ammon shook his head sadly again. Beth grabbed his hand and squeezed. "You should have let us go with you," she cried.

Ammon pulled away, walked toward a white couch, and fell back wearily. "I'm sorry," he muttered, "but he is gone, and there's nothing any of us can do."

Beth sighed in despair, then glanced toward Luke, knowing he would be crushed. Ammon watched her and they exchanged a quick look before she turned away.

Luke missed the exchange as he moved to stand in front of Ammon. "Tell me what happened. Did you see *anyone?*" he demanded.

"I talked with Master Balaam," Ammon answered. Luke cringed, looked surprised, then cast his eyes to the floor.

Elizabeth sucked in her breath. "Master Balaam!" she muttered in astonishment. "He's over there? But he was the chancellor! He had everything! Look what he is giving up! It doesn't make any sense." Luke remained silent, and Beth took a step toward him and studied his face. He couldn't meet her eyes, and she covered her mouth. "Luke, you knew about Balaam?" she asked in a soft voice.

"Ammon told me a few days ago," he replied, then looked away, afraid of revealing his secret time spent with Balaam.

"But Master Balaam . . . !" she sighed.

Luke glanced over to Ammon. "Balaam has seen Sam, hasn't he?" he pressed.

Ammon was slow to answer. "Sam and Balaam are working together," he finally said.

"That's good!" Elizabeth exclaimed. "If the two of them are together, if Master Balaam is with Sam, maybe he will be able to—"

Ammon lifted a hand. "No, Beth, I'm sorry. Balaam isn't the same person you knew before. He isn't going to help Sam. Quite the opposite now. He is a demon, a monster, part of the reason Sam's there."

Beth looked away sadly, her eyes wet with tears. Luke bent

down to Ammon and stared into his face. The brothers stared at each other, as if reading each other's minds. "I'm tired, Luke," Ammon finally said as he pushed himself up. "I'm so tired. And weary. I don't know if I have ever quite felt like this before."

Luke nodded as he held out his hand to help his brother stand. "Ammon," he said as the two stood side by side, "before you go, there is one more thing."

Beth turned quickly around and took a step toward Luke. "Not now," she pleaded. "You need to give him time to rest."

"No, Beth, there is no time," Luke replied. "He needs to know Teancum was here."

Ammon looked up suddenly upon hearing Teancum's name. Teancum was a warrior, a man who knew no fear, a wild and impetuous fighter who was the first to defend. Ammon focused on Luke. "You talked to Teancum?" he asked.

"Yes. He came here looking for you."

"What did he want?"

"I don't know," Luke replied. "He wouldn't say." Luke thought back on Teancum's visit, remembering him stalking through the room, his long hair streaming back, his oversized white shirt flowing with each movement of his arms. He was agitated and anxious, restless as a cat in a cage. "He was very anxious to see you," he said to Ammon, thinking of Teancum's determined face. "Something is happening. You could see it in his eyes."

Ammon thought of the frenzy of the rally. Yes, something was happening. Events were speeding forward, and he had a momentary sense of spinning out of control. A darkness fell upon him, a black sense of frustration and defeat. He stared at his hands. He felt empty and hopeless.

"I'm so tired," he repeated, fighting the depression inside. "I'm so tired. I'm so tired. Let's talk later."

* * *

Time passed, and the battle with Satan grew more intense. As time went by, and as the battle grew more violent, Lucifer became more and more secretive, until he was rarely seen moving or working in the light. He became bitter and resentful, the anger and jealousy growing like a cancer inside. It ate him, cell by cell, maggots of hate feasting on his cankered soul, until after a time he was completely consumed by his rage. At times he was seen by his lieutenants to raise his fist to the light and curse the Father openly, threatening and spitting out hateful words of revenge until even his followers, even his former friends, avoided his presence, for he instilled loathing and fear.

But though his followers feared him and even resented his presence, still they were loyal, even devoted to him. He was their god now. He had promised them salvation, power, and revenge. He had promised them dominion over all eternity. And he would deliver. One way or another, they knew he would produce.

At one point, when a messenger came with particularly worrisome news, Lucifer fell in a heap of rage on the floor, writhing and groaning as if in great pain. He cried in frustration as his lips curled back, his eyes cold, almost yellow, the pupils constricting in anger. "I am the Begotten," he hissed in rage. "Worship me! Worship me!" He slapped his hands and feet on the floor.

The messenger fell back, a look of dread on his face, then moved out of the room before Lucifer could turn his temper on him. Lucifer slammed the door behind him and stalked sulkily, his steps fierce and angry as he paced through the room. Over time, he settled down, the fury subsiding into a manageable burn. He sat at his desk and scribbled instructions in a fierce, hurried hand. Then he called his lieutenants together and stood before them. "We have been too obvious," he sneered in giving his new instructions to them. "We've tried to beat him on the arguments, but that won't work anymore. We've got to change our tactics, or we fight a lost cause. We can't beat him straight up; he is too powerful.

"To get what we want we must be subtle as snakes; more deadly, more cunning, more patient, more mean. Think of the serpent, how it slithers through the garden. It's such a beautiful creature, slow and delicate, rarely seen but effective, low, and not loved, but gloriously efficient! The serpent is now our model; we must pattern our work after him. So go to your old friends and stand by their sides. Pretend you want to help them while whispering deceits in their ears. Only lie when you have to. Speak the truth when you can; for the truth, once it's twisted, is the most effective tool we have. Coat your lies with enough truth, and they will swallow it down.

"Now listen to me, people, for this is the key—evil can be twisted into virtue if you phrase it just right. Any vice is acceptable if you cloak it as an issue of freedom. Any immorality is worth fighting for if you tell them they are fighting for choice, if you wrap it in the mantle of privacy and freedom. So take their moral agency and turn it on them. But be patient . . . be patient . . . it takes time to turn the truth upside down."

The group murmured approvingly. Of course he was right! Lucifer frowned, then dismissed them with a sudden wave of his hand. "Go," he commanded. "We have much work to do!" His lieutenants fled his presence, anxious for relief from his hateful, yellow eyes.

* * *

As the Serpent fell into misery and darkness, Michael and his angels began to assemble and organize the army of God. They took strong men, the great leaders, and made them commanders over groups of hundreds and thousands and ten thousands. Then they set apart women and men to their callings, giving them power from God, and sent them out to bear testimony that Christ would provide their salvation *if* they would but have faith in him.

And so the great work of teaching and converting and saving the souls of men began.

As Michael began to proselytize among the children of God, preaching and teaching salvation and hope, he was saddened and surprised by the lack of response. Despite the mighty works, despite the miracles and proclamations of truth, despite the very presence of the Father and the pleadings of his Son, there were not enough who listened and believed. As would happen on the earth, the sad truth was that many of the Father's children were willing to stand and watch from the sides, interested but not committed, not willing to join hands with Satan, but also unwilling to dedicate themselves fully to the Son. Most would say the right things and go through the actions, but fewer were willing to make a commitment, and fewer still were willing to fight.

Lucifer watched Michael's growing army from afar, secure in his kingdom, knowing that none could disrupt him or rob him of his power as long as God's children were so slow to commit.

Then something happened that caused him to fear.

The righteous servants of the Lord began to come into his cities, working among his people and preaching the gospel there. They began to take away his followers, not many, but a few, even converting some of the souls Lucifer had fought for himself, including some he had fought very hard to bring to his side. And watching, the Serpent realized something he had not known before.

He couldn't stop the conversion if the messengers came.

He could throw up roadblocks, but that was all he could do. If the messengers of God chose to come, and if his people chose to listen, even the most hard-hearted could be swayed to God's side. There was no way to fight the testimonies that the messengers bore.

And this truth made him tremble with a feeling of weakness and fear.

So Lucifer adjusted his tactics, learning how to fight God by going to the source of his fears.

"Concentrate on the messengers!" he commanded his disciples. "Keep them from coming. Convince them to stay home. That is our only hope. It is hard to stop their conversion once it has begun. So you've got to stop the messengers, or they will destroy us all!"

* * *

Ammon walked by himself through the night. He had spent another fruitless day in search of his brother Sam, only to be rebuffed and finally compelled to flee for his safety.

How many days had he been searching now? How many times had he felt this frustration and dread, this hopeless, lonely feeling of losing someone he loved, someone he admired, someone who had cared about him. How many days? Ammon didn't know anymore. He was tired and lonely. He didn't know where to turn.

Ammon *knew* Sam was better than the decisions he'd made. But it didn't matter. He couldn't search anymore.

He walked absently, a weariness seeping into his soul, a deep sense of defeat and betrayal building inside. His brother! His own brother, a part of those people! They were so hateful, so foul! He could not understand.

It was the darkest part of the night, that quiet and brooding moment when the stars were beginning to fade, when the moon had just set but the purple of dawn was still nowhere on the horizon. The night wind barely stirred, and the smell of wet grass hung in the breeze, heavy with dew and the stillness of the quiet air, when Ammon finally reached the friendly streets near his home. He walked the city center, familiar and secure, but he took no comfort in the sights and smells of his home.

Stopping on a street corner, he realized where he was. The Great Capitol stood before him, a fortress of rock, majestic and tall, its spires reaching up to the stars, the white marble and granite illuminated as if by some internal light.

The Great Capitol was the highest and most beautiful building on the Central Square. The Capitol was huge, far larger than anything that would ever be conceived on earth. Enormous white marble spires reached up through the night; stretching skyward ten thousand feet to end in tiny points that glistened under the stars. Beautiful breastworks, bright and perfectly crafted in exquisite detail, accented the spires with glistening gold. The incredible building sat above the ground, suspended a hundred feet in the air. A great staircase of sparkling white stone reached up from the ground to the wide, wooden door. The staircase was empty. He saw no one there.

He stared at the structure while he suffered inside.

He missed his brother deeply: the feel of his hands and the look in his eyes, his good nature in the mornings (he was always in a good mood), the wave of his hair, and the strength of his word. Sam was strong. He had always been so. He had carried so many, so long and so far. Would all the good ones be taken early in this battle of life? Was there hope for any of them if men like Samuel could fall?

As Ammon struggled with his feelings, he suddenly sensed for the first time a feeling that was uncomfortable and entirely new. With a quiet *whoosh* it passed by him, making his heart skip a beat—a tiny brush, like a whisper, a tiny voice in his ear. *It's too late. There's no time. There's not a thing you can do!* He felt the passing of time and staggered suddenly back. He realized the moment was coming when it would be too late, when they would run out of time and there would be an end.

He sensed both the promise and darkness that passing time held in store. Yes, there was hope, but there was also great danger there.

And each was alone. Each was alone in his battle to find the worth of his soul, each alone in his battle to make the right choice.

Who could win in this conflict if not his brother Sam? Were they all destined to fail, to spend themselves in defeat, to waste their potential in a battle that couldn't be won? Was there no one who could help them? Were they all on their own? Sam, Master Balaam, and the others? Was there hope for anyone?

He took a deep breath as he stared at his feet. What was faith? What was hope? He didn't understand anymore.

Then he looked up and saw it—a yellow light in the Capitol casting a dim shadow there. He stepped back and stared. It took a moment before he understood what it was.

Michael was up there in his chamber, leading the battle for men. Michael and the others. So he wasn't alone.

Then Ammon thought of the weight that must press Michael down, the crushing responsibility of leading the war. He thought of the pain he must suffer, the sadness of watching so many turn away from the light, of seeing them hold their arms out to a darkness that would cut them in two. As Ammon stared at the window burning in the early morning light, he felt deeply grateful for Michael and the service he gave. He felt humble and thankful for the burden he bore.

Bless him, dear Father, he prayed in his heart, *for he carries a burden that I couldn't bear. When the dark angels scream, when the dark night falls near, let him know there are others who still pray for him.*

* * *

A thousand feet above Ammon's head, Michael worked alone in his chamber. As he hunched over his desk, his great shoulders sagged as if tremendous boulders had been placed on his back. He felt so discouraged and defeated, his entire soul combat-weary from the weight of the war. The battle had reached its pitch, and his emotions were raw as bare bone. Which side was winning? He didn't know anymore. So many had fallen, and more fell every day.

Michael pushed himself away from his desk, then bowed his head slowly and clenched his fists at his side. "How long must we fight them?" he cried from his soul. "How long must they suffer, and how many must fall?

"I'm growing so weary, dear Father, so weary, so tired. Strengthen me, Father, for I can't do this alone."

* * *

Far, far away, in a dark and quiet room that looked over a sullen and shadowy street, a room that was black, dull, and brooding and smelled of mold and old cloth, another man knelt hesitantly on the floor and prayed. He glanced around him quickly, knowing that if he were caught, his punishment would be swift and complete. Though he bowed his head slowly, he didn't dare close his eyes. His prayer was a whisper. "Father, I am a son wandering in a strange land. I am so far from home and I don't want to be here. I'm growing weary, dear Father, for I am all by myself. Please, don't forget me, Father, for I can't do this alone."

* * *

As dawn approached, Ammon found himself once again at his home. Entering quietly, he walked through the semi-darkness, feeling his way through the structure that was so familiar to him. A penetrating quiet had settled over the home, and he hesitated in the hallway, still restless but weary, unsure of what he should do. Turning, he made his way up the wide stairway to the octagon-shaped room on the top floor. There the walls and ceiling were tinted glass, allowing a perfect view of the landscape. He sat in the growing light, his eyes staring out, watching the transition from the shadows of night to the deep purples of dawn. He wrestled with the darkness, fighting the depression and fear that seemed to be building inside.

Sometime later, he heard a gentle knock, but before he could answer, the door swung open and a warm light filled the room. Jehovah paused at the doorway. Ammon stood immediately. "Brother!" he exclaimed, a look of joy on his face.

Jehovah glanced around, then nodded to the windows and the approaching morning. "It's beautiful, isn't it."

Ammon moved to his brother. "Yes, Brother, it is." He paused, then sputtered, "I'm so glad to see you."

Jehovah tilted his head, understanding. "I wanted to talk to you," he said.

Ammon took a step back. Jehovah moved to the nearest wall and studied the sky, then turned and glanced at the furnishings in the room. Nodding toward a white-framed painting sitting on a small stand near the far wall, he said, "Elizabeth is getting much better, isn't she."

Ammon glanced at the painting, a landscape watercolor in

pastel blues and pinks. "Yes," he answered. "I love all of her paintings, but she was particularly happy with this one."

Jehovah walked to the small painting and picked it up, examining it proudly. "I'm so pleased with her," he said, his voice full of pride. "She has worked so hard. And she is getting very good." He shot a knowing look to Ammon. "Can I tell you something about her?" he asked him as he smiled.

Ammon nodded anxiously.

"When Elizabeth first started painting, it was very difficult for her. But look at this now. Isn't it wonderful! Isn't it great how she does that: sets her mind to something, decides she's going to develop a talent, then works patiently, not embarrassed by her efforts, even if she starts out a little behind. When it comes to talents, I wish all of Father's children could be just a little more like Beth: not afraid of failing, not embarrassed for their weakness, not so prideful in their efforts to improve."

Ammon nodded agreement. Jehovah admired the painting for several minutes, turning it in various directions to catch the different shades of light. "It's wonderful!" he said finally. "I've got to tell her how pleased I am."

Satisfied, the Eldest Brother carefully replaced the painting on its three-legged display, then turned again. Ammon bowed and moved toward him, kneeling at his feet.

"Brother," Jehovah said, placing his hand on his head. "I know how you are feeling tonight. I understand completely what troubles you inside. And though I can't take this experience from you—it is part of the process, part of how you will learn—I can help ease your burden. You are sad and lonely; but I promise you, Ammon, that I will always be here for you. Keep working. Keep growing. Do the best that you can. And I promise I will be there when you feel you have nowhere to turn."

The Savior reached down and beckoned for Ammon to stand, then put his hands on his arms and squeezed gently. "You are strong, Ammon. You have broad shoulders and strong hands. I will need your shoulders to carry burdens, your hands to lift others up. I will need you to help me. Do you understand?"

Ammon nodded slowly. "Yes, Jehovah, I do."

"But remember this, Ammon. I won't ask you to do anything without being there too. I will never ask you to help me without being there to help you."

Ammon bowed again, his face already brightened, his worries already light. "Thank you," he said simply.

Jehovah squeezed once again. "Now, brother, there is to be an important council in the morning, and I want you there. Teancum will meet you. Look for him on the stairs. Come in the morning to the council, then you will understand a little better about what I need you to do."

* * *

Lucifer was alone in his chamber when one of his servants came to him, slipping through a half-open door. He sidled up to his master and whispered in his ear. "One of the new ones is causing me a little concern," the servant said.

"Which one?" Lucifer demanded.

"Samuel, the oldest brother of the four."

"What is he doing?" Lucifer asked.

"He was praying tonight, and that's not a good sign."

Lucifer cursed, looked away, then replied angrily, "He has been weak and indecisive since the day he arrived. I have never really liked him—he's too flighty, too free. But he is necessary, and I demand he stay here."

"Yes, my dear master. But there is something more."

"What is it?" he growled.

"Master, he is seeking out his old friends, those he used to know and be close to. Most of them, in fact all of his closest friends, are somewhere over here; they joined with us early—they were not hard to deceive. Now Samuel seems determined to make contact with them. He asks about them continually. In fact, he was asking lots of questions. I don't like it. And I don't like him."

Lucifer growled, the lines of his face growing tight.

The servant saw the rising anger in his master's eyes. "Master," he asked quietly, "what would you have us do?"

Lucifer turned toward him. "*Always* have someone near him," he commanded. "If it looks like Sam is having second thoughts, get a lie in his ear. 'It's too late,' you must tell him, 'you are already doomed. There is no repentance, not now, not for the likes of you.' Remember, my dear servant, it is in the nature of some to see the worst in other people, but some men only see the worst in themselves. Samuel is like this. He's acutely aware of his weakness. So you must take that weakness and turn it on him.

"So keep someone close. And keep those lies in his ear. And above all, you've got to keep him away from his friends. People are much easier to discourage if we can keep them alone. Our lies are more accepted when they are told in the dark. Sometimes isolation and loneliness are the best tools we have.

"Now, go! Keep him discouraged. Convince him there is no hope. Tell him that he is beyond redemption and there's no turning back. Tell him he can't be forgiven, and his family doesn't care about him anymore. Do these things, my faithful servant, and I promise you we will keep him under our control."

chapter eleven

The war council took place in the Great Capitol. The white marble spires reached up through the clouds, stretching skyward to end in tiny points that glistened in the bright summer light. Huge oval windows, symmetrically placed, looked out to the east upon the rising sun. The great staircase was crowded with people entering the building, an enormous and boisterous group of men and women who talked in urgent voices as they hurried up the stairs. There was a palatable sense of urgency in the air, a feeling of change, as if a day that had been long anticipated, though not looked forward to, was finally here. Among the crowd, leaders and messengers moved, their faces more intent than those who were not as aware.

Ammon paused outside the building, feeling his heart tremble as he stood at the stairs. A dazzling light shone from the upper windows, and he knew what it was. He took a deep breath, then began to climb.

Teancum was waiting at the top of the stairs. Ammon quickly found him in the crowd, for he was short and solidly built, his thick arms well-muscled under his tunic and white shirt.

Teancum moved toward him and extended his hand. The two young men shook, and Teancum stepped back. His hair was blond and full and he wore it in a mane at the back of his neck. He squinted his eyes at the sunlight, then tossed his head to push back a strand of long hair. There was something in the motion, something unruly and wild. He stood in front of Ammon with his thumbs jammed into a belt, his shoulders slightly crooked, a generous smile on his face. He carried himself with a certain attitude that Ammon instantly liked. This was a guy he could do business with. And there were rumors about him he wanted to know more about.

Grabbing Ammon's shoulders, Teancum pulled him away from the crowd. "Is it true?" he demanded in a low voice.

"True? Is what true?"

Teancum put his arm around Ammon's shoulders and pulled him tight, glancing around to keep their conspiracy to himself. "Come on, you know what I mean, Ammon," he prodded.

"I do? Are you sure?"

Teancum whistled. "Oh, I like that. No outright denial. Play dumb, kind of innocent, but not out-and-out stupid. I like that technique, use it all the time myself." He took half a step closer, "But listen, Ammon, you can tell me. Is it true what I heard?'

Ammon still didn't answer. "Teancum," he finally asked, "what are you talking about?"

Teancum rolled his eyes. "Did you go to their city? Did you go there alone?"

Ammon glanced around hesitantly, unsure whether he should be proud or ashamed. "Yes," he finally answered. "I've been there more than once."

Teancum whistled again and slapped him on the back. "Friend, you're either one of the bravest or dumbest guys that I know. And hey, don't get me wrong, either way is okay with me. You're my kind of guy, small brain but big heart." Teancum laughed, and that was good, because Ammon really didn't know if he had been serious before. Teancum looked around, then pulled him close again. "What were you looking for?" he prodded. "Spying on the 'great master'? Checking on his plans and strategies? Or did you go for the thrill, just to prove that you could?" Teancum lowered his voice to a whisper, as if confessing a sin. "Sometimes I do that, you know. Sometimes I just want to prove to myself that I can." He laughed gently and flashed that great smile again. "And you know what I figured out? The hunt is more fun when you know that the prey is bigger than you. So tell me now, why? Why did you go over there?"

"I went to find my brother," Ammon answered.

Teancum took a step back. "Your brother?" he said wonderingly. "And who would that be?"

Ammon started to explain, and as he did, Teancum's expression changed suddenly. "Samuel!" he sputtered. "You're Sam's little brother!"

"Yes, of course. You didn't know that?"

"No, I didn't make the connection. And why would I? There was nothing to tie the two of you together. But now . . . " He stopped and thought, then turned suddenly serious. "Listen to me, Ammon, there are a couple things about your brother you don't understand. And I need you to trust me and just stay away. There are things going on, things you wouldn't understand. But trust me, please, you've got to leave it alone. Don't go for your brother. Don't go for anything. Please don't ask me any questions. Just do this, okay."

Ammon stared at him, dumbfounded. "He's my brother, Teancum. What do you expect me to do?"

"I'm asking you, Ammon, to leave him alone."

Ammon felt his anger rising. "Listen to me, Teancum. There's no way I'm going to sit here . . . " An enormous bell over their shoulders sounded the council to order. The bell was so loud that there was no way they could talk as it rang.

"Ammon," Teancum pleaded as the sound drifted away. "For the sake of your brother, you've got to leave this alone. It's what he would want. I'm not lying to you." The bell rang again, sounding over the great city. Teancum glanced up, then turned for the enormous door. "Now, quick, we must hurry. The council begins."

Ammon stood there incredulous, but Teancum was already walking away. He hesitated, then followed, pushing through the bustling crowd.

They entered the main chamber, a huge, open room of pure and perfectly white granite. The stone walls were shaved to the thickness of paper, and they let the bright morning light seep in, bathing the room in a glorious glow. The ceiling was so high and the rock cut so thin that it took on the same hue as the sky overhead, a gorgeous deep blue that seemed to reach into space. An escort led Ammon to a far corner of the room, near the back wall, and he sat on a chair near a great white column of gray stone. The leaders and many other valiant ones gathered in the room. The Father was there, sitting upon his heavenly throne, his majesty and power beyond what words could describe, his beauty and compassion adding a perfect warmth to a face that was white beyond even the brightness of the sun. The Savior stood before him, wrapped in a simple white robe. His face was young and flawless, though his spirit body was less majestic than the Father's, his glory less bright, for he had not yet been perfected. That event would take place at a foreordained time that was a central part of the plan.

Jehovah, the Firstborn, the oldest spirit child of God, moved a step closer to the Father. Ammon could see in the gravity of his expression the burden he carried of fashioning the salvation of men. Michael the Archangel—he who would be given dominion over all earthly things, he who would be the first father to teach the first generations of men—stood at Jehovah's side, his brother and friend. Many spirit children, a mix of both women and men, filled the vast chamber; these were the spirits of the mighty, those who had been faithful in their testimony of Christ and had never wavered. The radiance of the Father reflected in their young faces. The mood was somber, even poignant, with a tinge of uncertainty in the air.

Ammon looked quickly around, searching the enormous room. He saw her near the front, but off to the side of the throne. He looked on her face, then cast his eyes to the stone floor. It broke his heart to see her and the pain that she bore. He wanted to run to her and stand at her side. But he knew that he couldn't. This was a scene she had to endure on her own.

* * *

She sat alone, to the side of the mighty chamber, a white sash wrapped about her shoulders, her hair pulled back in a ribbon, her face majestic, her eyes bright and passionate. Every person in the room was aware she was there, though few dared glance toward her and, out of reverence, none held her eyes.

Those who had the privilege of seeing her face, those who had the pleasure of speaking with her—they knew in their hearts that she was the most magnificent thing to grace eternity. Nothing in the universe would ever compare. Her beauty and majesty, her love and sweet smile were more than mere man could ever endure. Even the moon and the stars would hide their face when she passed, for the light they reflected was but a reflection of her.

She listened to the entire proceedings, her face intent and alive.

And though she had known it would happen, still it caused her great pain, sometimes even more than she thought she could bear.

* * *

The war council had been called for only one purpose: Lucifer had to be dealt with. The time of conflict had come.

At the Father's request, Jehovah conducted the council, a duty that he dreaded but performed all the same, for as in all things he sought do the Father's will, completely supplanting his personal desires to the concept of "Thy will be done."

Every spirit bowed as Jehovah moved to the head of the room.

Because it was a council and not a time of instruction from God, others had been invited to speak, a well-established pattern that would be followed on the physical earth. The council was organized, with witnesses prepared to testify for both sides. Six of the quorum were assigned to speak on Lucifer's behalf, to prevent insult or injustice in the council; six were assigned to represent the interest of God. One chair sat empty in the center of the room, for though the Deceiver had been invited, he had angrily declined to appear.

Peter, the chief of the twelve, took to the stand to describe the charges against Lucifer. He spoke with power and eloquence, quoting great words that were familiar to all, some of which had been known since the beginning of time and would seep into the next world to be held as the standard around which great nations would rise.

"We hold these truths to be self-evident: All of God's children are created equal, and all are endowed by our Father with certain unalienable rights. And whereas eternal principles guarantee that every person may act according to the moral agency which the Father has given, that all may be accountable for their own sins in the day of judgment, the constitution of the government of God's family has been established under the direction of God.

"And whereas the Accused has sought to usurp this constitution, to defile its intent, and destroy the agency of men, to bind them down to him through deception and lies;

"And whereas the Accused has sought, through both spiritual violence and sophistry, to capture and hold in bondage the souls of all men, and is now in open rebellion against the societies and order of God, this council has been convened to defend this constitution which we hold most dear."

As Peter read the charges against Lucifer, the enormous chamber remained deadly still. Everyone knew what the charges would be, for there were no more secrets among the children of God, and the evidence was damning, entirely whole, and complete.

Satan was indeed in open rebellion. He was seeking not only to destroy the souls of all who would follow, but to bring down and destroy the society of the Father, to take His kingdom and power and glory and claim it all for his own.

And because it was evident, and because he no longer denied it, there was no doubt of the outcome of the Council of God.

Lucifer had to be defeated, his rebellion disbanded or crushed. He could not be reasoned with. There was no common ground. His followers had to give up their sedition and quit converting God's children to their dark paths or be cast out and expelled from the presence of God.

Ammon shivered as he listened to the words Jehovah read. Damned for eternity. Denied their second estate. Cast out, never to be with the Father again.

The Father had spoken. A hush fell over the room. Jehovah and Michael were then tasked to see that his will was done.

* * *

She knew what the verdict would be, for time and the future were not a secret to her. And though she had had all of eternity to prepare for this moment, still, like any mother, it cut her to the soul. She pulled the white sash about her, stood, and walked from the great hall. She found her private chamber and hid her face to cry, almost falling in agony onto the stone floor. Her shoulders heaved as she wept, her heart so torn and pain-filled she didn't know if she could endure, her suffering so real it was a physical torment inside. She felt her heart breaking, a pain so exquisite that only a mother could bear. She wept for the Son of the Morning, for the great one she had loved. But she also wept for the others, her beautiful daughters, her magnificent and yet prideful sons. So many of her children! How could they reject her this way? Her goodness and mercy, her kindness and love. She had offered everything to them, everything that she had. She would have sacrificed anything, even her oldest son. She would have paid any price to keep them in the fold.

But they wouldn't. They didn't love her enough. Or they loved Lucifer more.

So she wept for the lost ones and the ones who would fall, for all those who would follow him into hell, for those who would betray the Father and betray her as well.

And when she wept, all of eternity, from beginning to end, every living creature and thing, bowed and wept for her pain.

The Heavens wept while she suffered, for all good things loved her.

chapter twelve

At the war council's end, the crowd began to disassemble, a reverent hush of silence still holding the Great Hall.

Ammon stood still in awe of the moment, then began to move toward the main door when something caught his eye. He looked up to see Michael motioning toward him from the front of the room. Ammon hesitated, then swallowed and walked toward him.

Michael the Archangel waited for Ammon and extended his hand. His eyes were penetrating and blue, dark as deep water, soft and kind, but clearly strong and determined, and Ammon saw a nearly overwhelming strength and purpose in his eyes. His white robe draped perfectly over his shoulders, and his bare chest and arms were dark and well defined. He stood tall and confident and full of energy, his magnificent presence commanding respect. The throng pushed around them, and Ammon was suddenly aware of the hurried voices and press of the crowd, but Michael seemed to ignore them, focusing his attention on Ammon, and for one powerful moment it was almost as if the two men were alone. A great comfort swept through Ammon, and he felt a sudden sense of peace. Michael smiled, almost winking, and said, "Thank you for coming, Ammon. It was kind of you to take the time."

"Michael, I am honored," Ammon replied humbly.

"If you have a few minutes," Michael said, "I would like to talk to you."

Ammon bowed at his waist. "Of course," he replied.

Michael pointed to a stairway. "Come then. Follow me."

The two men climbed, Michael walking in silence, Ammon following a few steps behind. After many, many stairs, they emerged at the top of one of the Great Capitol's corner spires and stood on a small stone platform ten thousand feet in the air. The platform upon which they stood was no more than ten feet square, and it dropped off vertically to the city below. The view was incredible, with the city center at their feet, the mountains directly before them, and the great lake at their back. There was no guardrail around the side of the small platform, but neither man seemed unnerved by the height at which they stood. A gusting wind blew, and Ammon stepped forward and closed his eyes, taking in the smell and feel of the air. Michael lifted his arms as if to embrace the wind. "This is one of my favorite places," he said in a low voice.

Ammon only nodded. No words could add to the scene that lay at their feet. Michael pointed toward one of the rocky peaks immediately to the west of the city. "I see you sometimes, sitting up there," he said. "You seem to be fearless. I admire how you climb."

Ammon shrugged self-consciously. "I like it up there. It's the one place I seem to feel the most peace."

"I sometimes wish I could join you," Michael whispered slowly, almost as if he were talking to himself. "I sometimes wish I could sit on the mountains and not have to think, not have to make so many decisions. I sometimes wish I could just . . . " His voice trailed off and he suddenly sighed, then shrugged. He glanced toward Ammon, then lifted his hand and pointed toward the city below, which spread out before them almost as far as their eyes could see. The streets were crowded with people for, as always, there was a great activity there. "Do you see them all?" he asked Ammon, pointing at the people below. "How many are down there? A hundred million in the city? And how many more can't we see?"

Ammon stared at the city. There were so many people. God's children could be seen everywhere.

Michael swept his arms again, then turned to Ammon and said, "Take any ten thousand people. Any ten thousand you choose. Of those ten thousand, how many do you think will fight for our cause?"

Ammon shook his head. "I don't know, Michael," he said.

"I have learned from experience the number is few. Many of our brothers and sisters are simply not that interested in the battle for good. Many will pretend and say the right words; some will commit, but then quickly fall away; others will go through the motions only to please their family or friends. But in the end, when it's over, few will have the faith to make the sacrifices that are required to stand next to Christ."

"But once we enter mortality . . . ?"

"It will only get worse. Believe me, dear Ammon, it will only get worse. The challenge of mortality is almost impossible for us in this world to really comprehend. Once we enter the physical world, it will be more of the same, only more bitter and ugly, with more opportunity to fall. Just like here, there will be those who claim to believe, but few will be truly converted. And those who are, those who are actually willing to fight, those who are willing to turn their faith into works, to get down in the trenches and serve their fellowman—we are going to need them, Ammon. We're going to need every one. We are so far outnumbered, the noble and great ones will have a colossal work to do.

"So those who are most valiant in this premortal world will be given a mission when their time on earth comes."

"Of course," Ammon answered as he stared into space. "You mean like those who have been selected be a prophet or great leader."

"Yes," Michael answered. "There are those, of course. But there are other things, equally noble tasks that we need others to do. Some will be sent as pioneers and given the responsibility of finding the truth, of introducing their family to the gospel so as to better the lives of generations yet to be born. Some will be sent at a time when the gospel is not on the earth, but they will be asked to fight for freedom, even to sacrifice their lives for the principles embodied in our constitution. Some will fight to free a land, others to keep a land free. And we cannot underestimate the power of those who will set an example, of being a light in a dark and dreary world. It is difficult for us to understand the impact these examples will have—small acts of kindness, a kind word, a fair deal, holding a dying hand, or lifting a little child whose parents refuse to lift them. Some will be tasked to take the gospel unto the world, many times for no other reason than to find a single individual and bring them the truth. Others will be born in a quiet and unobtrusive corner of the world, an island, a mountain village, a quiet city block, with a mission to protect their families and children from the evil in the world.

"So you see, Ammon, a great number of the valiant, the warriors for God, will be saved for the last days, before Jehovah reigns on the earth, when the battle between good and evil is dark and undecided, when the righteous are sorely tried because of the good they will do, and the evil outnumber them and seem far more powerful."

Ammon's mind drifted to Elizabeth. "Beth is one of those righteous ones," he said proudly. "She has already been told when she will enter mortality. And she has already made a promise, a sacred covenant with God."

Michael smiled knowingly. "Yes, Ammon, the time and circumstances of our condition on earth are revealed to us in the Father's time and in his own way. Some learn their mission early, for they must have time to prepare, while others might not be told until they are ready to go down to earth.

"And you're right, Beth has been chosen and set apart for a specific task, an incredible challenge that will not be easy for her. But what she will do, if she's successful, will impact many people in the last days. Indeed, it has potential to change the direction of an entire nation."

Ammon paused and wondered as a light shiver ran down his spine. Michael watched him carefully, seemingly reading his mind. He beamed, a dazzling smile of certainty and great confidence. "Remember, my dear friend," he said as Ammon stood in silence, "out of small acts of courage, the Father will accomplish great and terrible things. And the promises we make before we are sent to earth, the covenants we make with the Father here in the premortal world, will impact our actions in mortality in ways that will not be revealed."

Ammon turned to Michael. "You have made the right choice. Beth has always been valiant. She has always been strong."

"And so have you," Michael answered. "You are humble, just like Moses, and that's one thing that makes you so powerful. You understand the eternity that exists between yourself and the Father, but you also have the faith to see what you can become. And so you will be given a great responsibility. You will also make covenants with God."

"I don't need to be a hero. That's not something I need. All I want is to go down and be worthy to come back again."

"That may be all you want, but is that all God wants from you? Is that the only thing that matters, what *you* need to be satisfied?"

Ammon pressed his lips and stared at his hands. He would do anything, and surely Michael knew that was true.

Michael walked to the edge of the platform, then motioned to Ammon, and he followed to stand at his side. The sun was rising high, and a summer wind blew. Michael pointed to the city. "You said you didn't have to be a hero," he said. "That is an interesting word. Your world will have plenty of heroes, or at least that is what they will be called. But they will be amoral and selfish and so evil and foreign to your experience here that it's impossible for me to describe. Fame, lust, and money will be all they desire. And they will not be heroes, not in the real sense of the word. They will be famous and wealthy, but their riches will die with them.

"But I want you to know, there *will be* real heroes there. In the time you will live, there will be heroes around. Simple men, honest men who work two jobs, go to school, raise a family, and serve our God. An older couple who have the courage to seek out the truth while enduring the scorn and ridicule of their children and friends. A young man, a special spirit, who will take on a body that is deformed—and yet you will never see him unhappy or without a smile on his face. A young mother who will care for a daughter while she suffers a painful death, and yet never doubt or lose faith that her Father loves them both.

"Yes, Ammon, in your world famous people may be hard to find. But you will be surrounded by heroes, you will meet them every day. They will be the simple people who struggle but never give up, those who strive to be happy despite the cares of the physical world, those who dream of the day when they will find the truth, those who search for understanding as to why they were born, why there is pain, or what it all means, and yet continue to endure, knowing in their soul, somewhere deep inside, that there has to be an answer.

"These are the heroes that our Father needs down on earth. And you will be a hero. We already know that."

Ammon thought a long moment. There was so much he didn't understand, so many things about earth-life that were not clear to him. But he didn't question Michael. He was satisfied to listen and learn and remember what he said.

Michael looked him directly in the eye and concluded. "Because of the progress and decision you have made, because of the sacrifices you have endured, the talents you have developed, and the lessons you've mastered, you have been selected to be a leader among the children of men at a time when the fulness of the gospel will be on the earth. The plans were laid even before the Great Council was held, and you have been selected to be sent to earth at a very special time, a time when evil and hate will rage in the hearts of all men. It will be a fearful time, yes, but also a time of great promise. And you will have a mission, a specific service you will be asked to perform. You've got to start preparing now or you will not be ready."

Ammon stared out over the valley, a faraway look on his face. He watched the swirling wind blow across the huge lake, cutting ripples in random patterns on the surface of the water. His mind, like the wind, seemed to whirl in confusion. A thousand questions rolled inside him. Where did he even start? "But there's so much I don't understand," he started to say.

"It will come in good time. Be patient, and remember, it is all a part of the great plan."

Ammon shook his head. "But if I could just . . . "

"It will come, Ammon. Be patient. Have faith. And don't

let the things that you don't know detract from those things that you do. Stay the course, keep your faith, and you will figure it out."

Ammon pressed his lips, forcing restraint. The great angel turned away from the younger man and fell silent as he thought. Michael watched the busy city below, then shook his shoulders and said, "Time grows short for me now and I really must go. But there is one more thing that we have to discuss. And this is important. In fact, my young friend, it is the reason that I brought you here."

Ammon straightened himself, becoming even more intent. Michael leaned toward him and said, "I'm very worried about your brother. I'm afraid he might fall."

Ammon nodded sadly. "I have tried everything. But Samuel won't even see me."

"I'm not talking about Samuel. That's not who I'm worried about."

Ammon stared at him, confused, and Michael lowered his voice. "Do you remember your dream about the schoolyard?" he asked.

Ammon stepped back in surprise, then slowly nodded his head.

"Do you understand the dream?"

Ammon shook his head no.

"The man in the window was our Father. He is counting on us to help each other, for he can't do it himself; he can't intervene directly, even here in the premortal world. We have to learn to help each other and to trust others besides God. Even here, even now, the lessons of eternity must be taught, and Father is counting on us to help save his children, to lift each other up at the times when we fall. And remember, Ammon, most of the prayers people utter will be answered by what someone else does. That is true now, and will be even more true in the mortal world."

Ammon thought back on the dream. It made so much sense to him now. "But there was this boy, a little child . . . "

"Do you know who that was?"

"No! I never could see his face."

Michael's eyes softened as a look of grief crossed his face. "It was Luke. Oh my Luke—he is the one the Father is concerned about now. His heart is so good, but he is tender and flexible, like a young reed in the wind; he wants the right thing, but he is so vulnerable. And he needs you now, Ammon, even more than you know. And you may have only one chance to save him before it's too late."

chapter thirteen

Later that morning, after the council and his conversation with Michael, Ammon found Luke and Elizabeth in a park near their home. The day was warm and pleasant, with a whiff of distant rain in the air. The common area was enormous, a huge quad of perfectly manicured grass and tall, swaying trees. A million flowers had been planted in beautiful gardens along the side of a pond and they were now in full bloom, for spring was wearing on and summer was near.

Elizabeth and Luke gathered around Ammon, anxious to hear everything. Beth was so excited, she could barely contain herself. Michael the Archangel! The Council of God! She had heard rumors already, and she wanted to know it all. She sat on a small marble bench in a simple white and blue dress. Luke remained standing, shifting uneasily from one foot to the other while Ammon sat on the grass, resting back on his hands. Elizabeth leaned forward and crossed her ankles. "What was Michael like?" she asked excitedly. "What did he say to you?"

"Tell of the council first," Luke interrupted. "What did Father decide?"

Ammon told them of the decision arrived at in the council. Luke nodded solemnly, but didn't say anything. Elizabeth gasped when he told her; just the thought, just the threat of being cast out took her breath away, and it was inconceivable to her that it had come to this. A shiver ran through her, and she tucked her arms to her chest. "What about Michael?" she then wondered. "Why did he send for you?"

Ammon told them of their conversation. But he did not tell them all. His voice remained firm and even, but as he glanced toward his younger brother, as he thought of Michael's warning and the dream he had had, he fell silent a moment as the emotion rose in his chest.

He heard Michael's voice. *Luke. Oh my Luke—he is the one the Father is concerned about now.*

Luke watched him, knowing that something was wrong. He knew his older brother as well as he knew himself; he could read his body language and the look in his eye. He could tell what he was thinking by the sound of his voice, reading his emotions by his inflection and tone. And something was wrong—there was no doubt in his mind. He watched him a moment, uneasiness building inside. "Did Michael say anything else?" he prodded gently.

Ammon glanced toward him, then looked away. Elizabeth and Luke waited patiently, then realized Ammon wasn't going to say more.

"I'm a little surprised that Michael took so much time with you," Luke stated. "He is so busy! Why did he have to talk to you about the need for valiant spirits and the mortal mission you'll have? Why was it important to tell you that now?"

Turning to Luke, Michael's voice rolled again in Ammon's

mind. *Luke. Oh my Luke—he is the one the Father is concerned about now.* He shook his head to clear it, then answered quietly, "At first, I was asking myself the same thing, Luke. But it makes sense to me now. He is very busy, yes; in fact, there were others he had sent for, other men, just like me. But what we talked about was important, so I'm not so surprised now."

Elizabeth stared at Luke. Had he missed the whole point? "I'm not surprised at all," she answered quickly. "I mean, this is what Michael does. This is how he fights for men's souls. One-by-one. One-on-one. Convert and strengthen one person, then send him or her to bring others home. So no, it doesn't surprise me he wanted to talk to Ammon. We too are important."

Luke thought a moment. "You are right," he conceded. "I should have seen that myself."

The three young people fell silent, each of them lost in private thoughts. Luke watched his older brother, then asked, "Do you think there is anything we can do for Sam?"

Ammon brought his hands to his chin and closed his eyes. "Michael didn't offer any suggestions for what we might do," he replied.

"But we've got to do something, Ammon!" Luke said. "Sam loves you. He respects you. I am too young. You know he won't listen to me. I would go and try to find him myself, but I can't do this alone. I'm just the youngest brother. Sam won't listen to me."

"What can we do?" Ammon asked.

"I don't know. . . . Talk to him. . . . See if you can make him see."

"You've got to understand, Luke," Ammon answered. "I've thought about this for days; I've thought of almost nothing else since the day he left. But I really don't know. . . .

It's not like we can force him. We can't *make* him come back."

"Look," Luke shot back, his voice edged with anger. "Sam isn't stupid. He knows what he's done. And he had good reasons for his decision. He isn't evil or mean. He didn't do what he's done to hurt us, you know. He did what he thought was right, not what he knew to be wrong."

Ammon pushed himself up and took a step toward Luke. His voice remained calm, though his face brushed in pain. "I didn't say Samuel was evil. I've never thought that in my life. But he has to take responsibility for what he has done. And we both have to realize that we might run out of time. Father won't allow this battle to wear on forever, and there will come a time when Sam might be found on the wrong side. And if that happens, it will be his choice. We can't force him to come home."

Luke stepped back and shook his head. "What will happen to him?" he cried, brushing his hands through his hair.

"I don't know, Luke. I don't know."

The three fell silent again until Elizabeth spoke. "He could die," she whispered sadly.

"This is not mortality," Ammon shot back. "There is no death here."

"There is spiritual death. Separation from God. That is the only death that matters, and that is possible now."

Ammon started to answer, then cut himself short. Beth looked across the lawn as the wind caught her hair, feathering the dark strands behind her ears. Ammon rocked on his feet and stared at the grass. "Sam is in mortal danger; there is no doubt in my mind. He might lose the opportunity to take on a physical body. Many have gone after Lucifer and never come back."

"Maybe if you talked to Master Balaam again?" Luke suggested.

"No. He will never help us. If you had seen Balaam and the glare in his eye—there is a physical change, he looks different somehow, angry and grim. His face is dark, his smile evil. He looks almost . . . distorted. It is hard for me to explain, but he looks almost . . . *fallen* is the only word I can use to describe it, but the battle scars are ugly when you are fighting for the wrong side. And he isn't going to help us, I can assure you of that. And without Balaam's help we won't find Sam, at least not by ourselves."

"So we just—what—give up, stay here all warm and happy and say that we tried?"

"We did try," Ammon answered. "We did everything we could."

"But he needs us, Ammon. I can feel that right here!" Luke thumped his chest. "He is praying we will find him. He is praying that we won't give up."

Ammon's jaw clenched. "Sam doesn't pray anymore, Luke. I'm sorry, but that is the truth. He's had every opportunity, and he has turned us away. And if he refuses to see us, if he hides in the city and doesn't want to be found, there's just not much we can do . . . "

"We could try to . . . "

"To what, Luke? Try what? What do you want me to do?"

"I don't know, Ammon. I'm too young. I'm not like you and Beth; I don't hold the same promise. I'm not as smart, and I haven't developed the same talents and abilities as you. But I do know that Samuel is praying that we won't give up on him."

Ammon looked away. Elizabeth stepped to Luke's side and touched him on the arm. "It's not fair to get angry at Ammon," she said. "He didn't cause Sam to leave."

"I know that!" Luke cried in frustration and grief.

Ammon moved closer to Luke and put his arm around his shoulder. "We'll think of something," he offered. But it was clear in his voice that he didn't have much hope.

Luke shuddered as he trembled with frustration and fear. "I have always loved Jehovah," he said in a grieving voice. "He has been the perfect big brother. He is always there to talk to. He was always there to play games with us when we were small. Has he ever, even once, made us feel like he didn't have time? And how many times have we turned to him to draw on his strength? If I have ever felt overwhelmed, he has always been there.

"You know that I love Jehovah. But I love Samuel too. And now I feel like I'm in a situation where I have to choose between them.

"And that's not the only thing that I hate about this plan. I don't want Jehovah to suffer. If Lucifer wants all the glory, I say let him pay the price. If he is willing to suffer, if he brings us back, I say good for him. That seems pretty fair. Is that such a bad idea?"

Ammon stepped back and Elizabeth held her breath. "You didn't say that," she whispered. "What's the matter with you, Luke. Are you losing your senses?"

"Oh, so now I'm evil too! Crazy or evil, just like my brother Sam."

Beth began shaking, fighting to keep her emotions inside. Ammon stepped away, a look of surprise on his face. "What's the matter with you, Luke? What are you talking about?"

"I know what you're thinking," Luke was quick to reply. "If I don't fall in line, then I must be evil too! If I have the courage to question, or look at the other side, then I must either be crazy, or wicked like Sam. I know how you think. I have seen this before."

"Be quiet, Luke," Ammon said in an angry voice. "You're upset. Let it go. We can talk again later on."

"Oh, sure. Just hush up, little brother, you're not smart enough to talk. Well, let me tell you something, *big brother.* I've been talking to Master Balaam and he warned me you would react this way. I didn't believe him at first. I thought that you would still care; but it's obvious to me that you don't care about Sam. You only care about yourself and your high-powered friends. Too busy to bother! I see what's going on. Balaam told me this would happen, and now I see he was right."

Ammon looked at him, dumbfounded, as Luke stalked away.

* * *

Luke walked until darkness had settled over the great city, finding a lonely trail where he could be by himself. He wanted to get away, but he didn't know where. He wanted to think, but his mind was a cloud.

He walked for many hours, thinking, stewing, trying to sort it out. A torturous battle took place somewhere between his heart and his head, between the things he knew and the things that he felt.

He knew it was wrong. He had known that from the start—it was wrong and destructive. Yet, like a hot dripping acid he couldn't seem to turn off, the panic ate at him, consuming his soul until his fear of the future had complete control of him, his lack of faith filling him completely with indecision and dread.

All he wanted was for things to go back to how they had been before. Yet, when he looked at the future, only one thing was clear: they weren't strong enough, very few of them were. It was too dangerous, too risky. There had to be a better way.

As he walked through the darkness, not knowing where he could go, the blackness inside him seemed to only grow worse, the isolation more bitter, the anger more sharp.

He only wanted to protect them. Why were they such fools? They were his family! Must everything be so hard?

Oh, how he hated this feeling! He didn't want to feel this way anymore.

chapter fourteen

Lucifer sent for Balaam, sending word through a runner for him to report immediately. It took Balaam some time to get past the sentries and guards who had been placed to protect the master's new home, an imposing fortress on the side of the hill. Since the decision of the council, the security around the palace had become incredibly tight, for the master had made the jump from suspicion into the realm of paranoia and fear. Once past the sentries, Balaam was escorted into the Grand Hall, a magnificent corridor that took his breath away, an ostentatious and stunning display of power and greed. Bricks of gold and precious stones had been imbedded in the floor and glittering chandeliers hung eighty feet over his head. Exquisite crown moldings accented the exposed ceiling beams. The walls of the mighty corridor were beautifully painted with murals depicting Lucifer in his glory: a Son of the Morning, a hero in battle, and finally the coming of the great King. Concourses of angels were depicted singing praises to their lord, their arms raised in glory and worship to him. Balaam studied the mural as he walked slowly by, reading the words the angels would sing:

Glory to him who will save us
From Jehovah's bitter fall.
He will defend our salvation
Let the glory be his!
He will fight for our happiness
He will fight for our ease—
Why would they cheat him?
He only claims what is fair.
We love him
We praise him
Let the glory be his!

Passing the great mural, Balaam came to an enormous door, a solid piece of wood that was at least fifty feet high. As he drew near, it opened for him and he felt a cold breeze on his face. Lucifer was waiting on a magnificent throne, a huge and garish symbol of his ego and pride. The enormous arms were golden tiger paws, the four legs coiled snakes, the backrest jutting to an apex of diamonds that glittered like stars.

The servant, bent and terrified, approached the great master. He whimpered to please him, almost licking his hand. His eyes, red-rimmed and teary, flickered with a sullen yellow glow, the brighter light having burned out a long time before. "Master!" he whimpered. His great voice, once so compelling, once able to capture a listener with its rolling power, was hardly more than a sniffle, a hoarse and crackling sound.

Balaam had not talked with Lucifer for a very long time, but he had watched him from a distance. He had seen what he had become, and there was no doubt in his mind what Lucifer was capable of now. So Balaam approached him in fear. Bowing at his feet, he fell to his knees, unable to look upon his master's face. "Master," he repeated in a bootlicking tone.

Lucifer watched him a moment, then gave a sharp command. "Stand and look at me."

Balaam forced himself up and lifted his eyes. Looking upon Satan's face, he gasped and took a step back. The transition was complete now, and he shuddered inside. The once mighty leader, the Son of the Morning, was now but a shell of who he used to be. Gaunt and tired, he was now bent with anger and broken with rage. But though he now looked dark and evil, Balaam could also see that he was even more powerful, for there was a mighty force about him, an authority and energy that could not be denied. His priestcraft grew stronger with every soul he destroyed.

Balaam stepped back and Lucifer smiled. "So, Balaam," he said sarcastically. "Why do you look so surprised?"

"I'm sorry, great master. It's just that you look so . . . tired, sir. I hope you are well."

The Destroyer smiled bitterly, then drew himself together and lifted his voice. He stood up from the throne and pulled his shoulders square. His face shone with a light that seemed to emit from his eyes, casting a shadow over his cheeks and his nose. His skin grew more tight, his hair dark and full. He drew large and strong, his neck taunt, his chest tight. Power and beauty seemed to shimmer from his face, like a mirage in the distance on a hot, sultry day. Even his throne seemed to brighten, casting a golden light through the room. "I can be beautiful when I want to!" he boomed in a powerful voice. "I can still be an angel, a beautiful angel of light. I can deceive men when I need to, so don't you worry for me."

Balaam lowered his head and muttered an unintelligible reply. The master's light faded and he relaxed once again, seeming to draw into himself, as if shrinking with age. He pointed toward his servant. "Balaam," he said, "time precludes us from the pleasantries of rehashing old times. We are fully focused on the battle, and there is no time for that now."

"Yes, Master Mahan," Balaam replied.

"I have sent for you, Balaam, because of the promise you made. You made a vow to me, Balaam, and I haven't forgotten. And now comes the work that I need you to do."

Lucifer brought his hands together, lifting them over his head, then moved them in a circle, sweeping an arch through the air. "Look, Balaam," he commanded. "Look now and see the mission I have prepared for you."

Balaam kept his eyes on his master. The vision was opened, and he watched carefully.

"He is alone now," Lucifer said. "You can see his discouragement—look, there in his eyes. He hasn't spoken to Ammon or Elizabeth for more than three days. He is avoiding them, always seeking time by himself. He spends most of his time walking through the trails that line the foothills of their city. He thinks he is hurting, but it is really his pride. He isn't thinking of others; he thinks only of himself—his hurt, his anger, his sadness and confusion. He is so focused on his own pain that it's all he thinks about now. He assumes he is the only one to ever experience such disappointment or grief, and so it festers inside him, like a poison that eats at his heart. There, now you see, he is walking alone. I want you to go to him, Balaam, and convince him to come to me. Persuade him to listen. That's all I need; for if he entertains my ideas, I can get him, I know."

"Yes, Master Mahan. I serve at your will."

"Yes, of course you do, Balaam. Of course you do, friend. Now do this thing, Balaam, and you will get your reward. I will give you what I promised. You have my sacred word." Satan lied so easily, even he had trouble keeping track of the truth. He couldn't remember what he promised, but it made no difference to him. He would say what he needed to say to get the result he desired. "When I rule this world," he continued, "I will need men like you. And you will rise in great power if you do what I say. So do this for me, and you will have those things you desire."

* * *

Luke walked alone on the trail, his head down, his eyes focused on his feet, his heart weary with discouragement and anger and fear. Evening was coming on and, in the west, dark clouds grew, promising rain sometime in the next few hours.

As Luke walked, he heard a strange voice and lifted his head with a start. Balaam, the great teacher, the most celebrated and best-loved chancellor at the university, approached from a trail that ran through the trees to his right. "My young Luke!" he exclaimed as he stepped onto the road. "Luke, my dear Luke, how are you doing, boy?"

"Master Balaam," Luke answered quickly, hiding the surprise in his voice. He looked around carefully. "What are you doing here?"

Balaam folded his brilliantly colored robe around his waist, flipping it coolly with a twist of his hand. "I came to talk to you, dear Luke. I came to offer assurance . . . "

Luke cocked his head suspiciously. "I don't need your sympathy," he replied angrily.

"Of course you don't, Luke. Believe me, I know that better than you could ever know. You see, Luke, in many ways you and I are the same. We're not the kind of men who need sympathy or understanding. You don't need to be treated with kid gloves, not like Ammon always wants to do. And that's not what I'm here for. I came to talk, man-to-man, brother-to-brother. And all I ask is that you treat me with the same respect with which I intend to treat you."

Luke watched him a moment, then frowned, turned away, and started walking again. Balaam hesitated as Luke walked a few paces ahead. When he stopped and looked back, Balaam leaped to his side.

And with that, he knew that he had him. The master was right. He was weak and vulnerable.

* * *

Farther down the narrow road, behind a low-hanging bow of an ancient oak tree, Lucifer waited and watched. He turned his head to listen, anxious to hear every word. If Balaam were to fail, he was prepared to step in, though he greatly hoped that didn't happen, for it would be so much better if Luke chose to come by himself, if he chose to listen to Balaam without direct persuasion from Lucifer. Yet this was important, and he was ready to intervene, for he had learned from experience that sometimes God's children needed his personal touch—those special words, those exquisite lies that only he told so well.

As the two men approached, Lucifer pushed back, burying himself in the shadows of the ancient oak tree. He watched and listened from the shadows as the two men came to a stop.

"That is an exceptional robe you are wearing, Master Balaam," Luke said.

Balaam glanced down, then lifted his arms with great pride. "It's beautiful, isn't it. I have many like it. You see, we believe it is important to present yourself well. It is important to show others when you have attained a certain stature in life."

Luke admired the robe. "And you are happy now?" he asked with a tilt of his head.

"Oh yes, Luke, very happy. There is so much you don't know, so much you have never experienced. If I could only open your eyes to the many good things in life, to the many things we have been denied. The Father has many secrets, Luke, things he refuses to tell us, pleasures and joys he won't tell us about. He has great knowledge and powers that he keeps to himself. Did you know, for example, that there are fruits you have never experienced, luscious, lovely fruits you have never tasted before? And there are wonders you can't imagine regarding our spirits and minds, feelings and knowledge you have not considered before.

"And there is so much fun and excitement, I just wish I could explain. Surely there is more to life than work, you know. You have felt that before; I can see it in your eye. Work and drudgery. Work and school. Work and . . . " Balaam suddenly paused. "Well, you know what I mean, Luke. At least I suspect you do."

Luke didn't answer, and Balaam shook his head sadly. "You know, when I look back on it, I'm ashamed for myself. I used to be so hard on my pupils, used to push them so hard. Yet, in my single-minded desire to provide them more knowledge, there were so many pleasures I denied them. But those days are over. I'm not like that anymore, for I have discovered the meaning of real pleasure now."

Luke stared down the road, apparently uninterested. He pressed his lips together and breathed a deep sigh. In the shadows to his left, Lucifer cursed to himself. Balaam was on the wrong track. He needed to try something else.

Balaam shifted uncomfortably as silence hung in the air.

"I want to talk to Samuel," Luke said in a defiant tone. "You could take me to him. But I suspect that you won't."

"Of course you want to see him. And he wants to see you as well."

"Will you let me see him?" Luke demanded.

"How could I stop you? You are free to do what you choose."

"But you wouldn't let Ammon see him."

"Sam didn't want to see him, and truthfully, Ammon didn't try very hard. He asked once or twice, but that was about all. I suspect he was more interested in putting on a show, being able to say he had tried, than in actually getting through."

"But you think he will see me?"

"Of course he will, Luke. He misses you so!"

"When? Where? I want to see him right now!"

Balaam shrugged casually. "In time, Luke, in time. He is very busy right now."

"I don't want to wait."

"Of course you don't, Luke. As I said, he is busy. But you will get to see him. I promise you will."

Balaam turned away from Luke and started walking again. Luke hesitated a few seconds, then rushed to catch up. "You know," Balaam said as Luke moved to his side, "your oldest brother and I seem to think the same way. All Sam wanted was the freedom to act for himself, the freedom to have a little fun and not be so tied down. He feels we shouldn't be forced to follow the same path, that we shouldn't have to act the same, dress the same, even talk and think the same way. He feels a great need for freedom, a need to not be tied to one plan.

"And think about that, Luke. Under our plan, no one will ever call you lazy or rebellious or evil. No one will ever pass judgment on the way you look, dress, or feel. And there won't be this constant divisiveness, this constant conflict and *strife.* I'm so tired of it, Luke, and I'm sure you are too. I mean, haven't you noticed how intolerant those who follow Jehovah have become? They refuse to include us, but instead threaten to cast us out, and all because we don't agree with *everything* they say. They have become a group of bigots and extremists; intolerant and close-minded fools, unwilling to even consider that we might have a point. And I'm so tired of them trying to force their values on us, shove their religion down our throats, the way they chip away every day at our freedom of choice. I say live and let live. Is that too much to ask?"

Luke was slow to answer. "I'm so tired of the contention. I don't want to talk anymore. All I want to do is see Samuel," he replied as they walked.

"And I will take you to him. But not for a while. We have other things to talk about, other things we have to do first."

Luke thought a long moment, his face weary and tight. "I just don't know anymore," he finally mumbled to himself.

"Then come and listen," Balaam cried. "That is all I ask. Just come and listen to his plan. Is there any danger in that? You don't have to decide. What are you hiding from? Lucifer isn't such a bad man; you have seen that yourself. He's good and caring, and he is so strong and smart. I'm only asking that you listen long enough to see what he can offer you."

"I don't know . . . I just don't know. I need to talk to Ammon, I guess."

Balaam's heart jumped. That was the last thing in the world he wanted Luke to do. "No, Luke!" he replied, barely hiding the panic in his voice. "You already know what Ammon will say. I mean, could anyone be any more predictable? And aren't you a man? Aren't you capable of making a decision yourself? I think you are. Now come on; let's go."

"But I can't just leave them. That's what Sam did, and you know how much that hurt everybody. I owe it to them to at least try to explain."

Balaam thought, then reached into his robe and pulled out a tightly folded piece of brown paper. "I agree with you, Luke, but there is a better way. Let's write a note. I can help you explain. It will be easier for both you and them if we do it this way. Now come—it is late, and we've a long way to go."

chapter fifteen

It was very dark out and very late at night when Balaam and Luke were escorted down the Great Hall and through the high wooden door. Outside the air was heavy, smothering, a blanket of heat kept down by the smoke and haze in the sky. Inside the Great Hall it felt the same way: stale and lifeless, with a tinge of dry smoke in the air.

The Great Hall was dimly lit, and once again, the door opened as they approached. Entering the inner chamber, they found Lucifer waiting, his smile so wide it was clearly contrived. He had cloaked himself in an exquisite white robe with long, flowing tails and full, sweeping sleeves. Atop his dark hair, he wore a glass crown, its silver spires sitting like spikes on his head. He looked simply magnificent, surrounded by his power and wealth, and Luke couldn't help but bow as he approached the great master, for his surroundings were so overwhelming he felt entirely compelled.

Lucifer loosened his smile and extended his hand. "Luke, I'm so glad you came. I think so much of your brother. It's good to finally meet you."

Luke didn't answer as his throat choked a bit. Lucifer

watched him a moment, studying him carefully. He looked deep in Luke's eyes, seeing the tenderness there, then made a quick decision, knowing what he had to do.

"Luke," he said simply. "I'm a busy man, and I'm sure you are too. So let me cut to the heart of the matter, if you will.

"First, I want you to know that I have watched and observed you for a very long time. And I know how you think. I know how you feel. I know what motivates you—and it isn't power or greed. You are a good person, Luke, with a soft spot in your heart."

Luke stood without moving as the Deceiver walked to his side and put his arms around him, drawing the younger man close. "This is the way I see it," Lucifer continued. "You love your brothers and sister. And you are happy here. Maybe we aren't like the Father, but how important is that, really? We have each other and this world—what a wonderful place! So why does it have to change, you wonder. Why do we have to go through all this suffering now? And it bothers you, Luke, that it will only get worse. Am I right there, young man? Is that about how you feel?"

"Yes," Luke answered slowly, his voice barely escaping his throat. He felt a cold chill around him, a chill that seeped to his bones. He stared straight ahead as Lucifer pulled him close again.

"You love your sister, don't you, Luke? In fact, I would say that you love her more than any other thing in this world."

Luke only nodded as an image of Beth seemed to leap in his mind. He saw her resting on a white pillow, her face peaceful and serene. The image was so real he thought it actually was real, and he wondered if Lucifer had opened a portal to her.

Lucifer watched him react from the image he had planted

in his mind. "Do you realize," he continued, "what is going to happen to Beth?"

Luke looked at him suddenly. "What do you mean?" he asked.

"Do you realize what is going to happen to your sister when she goes down to earth?"

"There is no way I could know. We are not shown the future; that is a part of the plan. But she did say that . . . "

"That she has been given a mission. And it won't be easy for her. Isn't that right, Luke? Isn't that what she said?"

Luke nodded sadly. "Yes, she said it would be difficult. But she is also excited."

Lucifer laughed bitterly. "Of course she's excited. Why would she not be excited when she is kept in the dark? It's easy to keep the masses happy when they are kept unaware and filled with ignorance. But she has no idea what pain lies in store. She doesn't understand the heartache she will have to endure. If she had any idea, believe me, she wouldn't go."

Luke tried to pull back, but Lucifer held him close. Leaning into him, Lucifer put his lips close to his ear. "Let me show you, Luke," he whispered. "Let me show you what will happen to Beth. If I show you the pain she will suffer, maybe you can intervene and save her. If you could see the things she will have to go through on earth, perhaps you will see the wisdom of my plan. Once you see the pain those you love are going to suffer, it becomes easy to see that there is a much better way."

Luke couldn't seem to answer as Lucifer cast his spell. The master's voice was perfectly pleasant, so calm and assured. He was so tall and handsome, so confident and strong. And his cold arms around Luke seemed to support him somehow, sustaining him with answers when he didn't know what to do.

"Will you let me show you?" Lucifer asked again in that

perfect, sweet voice. It was so soothing, so mellow, and yet it pierced Luke to his soul. "Will you watch what I show you? Do you have the strength to know the hard truth?"

Luke nodded slowly. "Yes, I want to see."

Lucifer stood suddenly back and Luke felt his knees bend. He reached out for Lucifer, needing to steady himself.

"If I show you, do you understand that you will have to act?" Lucifer asked him, his voice more pointed now. "You can't sit idly by once you have seen the truth. You will have to do something to save her, to defeat this evil plan. You understand that, don't you, Luke? Once I show you the future, you will have to act."

Luke nodded slowly and Lucifer smiled. "Then look, my young friend. Look at what is in store. This is a vision of your sister's future and how she will suffer on earth. This is a vision of her future and what Jehovah will put her through."

The dark vision began to unfold. Luke saw the little girl, and though she was young, he knew immediately it was her, for she had the same eyes and the same beautiful smile. But she was dirty, sick, and hurting. And she was only a child. He watched the scene open as if he were standing there nearby. He watched and he listened, feeling sick in his heart.

* * *

The girl looked up with terrified eyes—wide, dark, and expressive, but showing only fear. Her father pulled her close, and she felt him shudder beside her. He took a deep breath. "Stay here," he whispered. He began to stand up as the sound of the vehicles drew close, the roar of their engines unmuffled by the hut's thin plywood walls. The child pulled on her father's fingers, not letting go. "Don't leave me, Father," she begged him. The father, himself very young, knelt on one knee and held his child at arm's length, looking her in the eye.

"I must go. I am village leader now that your grandfather is gone. And perhaps it isn't the soldiers. It has only been four days. I doubt they would be back to trouble us so soon."

The girl glanced at the sound of the approaching vehicles. Though only six, she was not fooled. She recognized the sound of the soldiers' trucks.

The rains had stopped just twenty minutes before, and a heavy mist hung from the jungle canopy, dripping and wet, misty fingers that sifted through the trees but never quite reached the ground. The fog moved silently, almost as if it were alive, searching for something among the tall leaves. The surrounding mountains cast shadows through the thick underbrush, bringing on darkness before the sun had fully set. Far in the distance, somewhere east of the river, the roll of thunder echoed back through the trees as the rain squall moved away, pushing up the mountains that lay to the east. The air was so thick it took effort to breathe, for the smell of death seemed to be everywhere. Four rotting goats lay near the village fire, their coats turning oily as the carcasses rotted from inside. Four days earlier, the command had been given to leave the dead goats where they were. "They will serve to remind you," the villagers had been told.

And now, only four days later, the soldiers were back. The army trucks sloshed to the center of the village and stopped. Beginning their work, the soldiers moved purposely among the trails and shacks. The murders took place in relative silence, with no screams of protest and few cries of pain, only the dull thud of weapons falling again and again. It was better to be silent, the villagers had learned, for there were worse things than dying and worse ways to die.

After four years of brutal oppression, the village had given up the battle for life. Their instinct for survival having been beaten away, the terrified villagers stood like cattle, huddled in submission. Their shallow eyes and sagging shoulders did all the talking for them.

The murder weapons were as primitive as the men who held them in their hands. Shovels, hammers, and iron rods—these were cheaper than bullets and effective enough. The tools were surprisingly tidy, the dull ends leaving few traces of blood, only bludgeoned, beaten bodies with purpled foreheads and broken necks. The carcasses littered the ground—four young men, two women, and three half-naked children. Their tangled bodies followed a line from the center of the village down the slope toward the river. The forest scavengers stood ready. They could be heard moving through the brush—lizards and rats and the greasy-feathered vultures that had learned to stay near the village where meat could most often be found.

The soldiers weren't truly soldiers—at least most of them weren't—but wild-eyed boys in ill-fitting uniforms, oversized jungle fatigues that draped over their bodies. The conscripts held their faces tight and tried to hide their trembling hands. Peasants and farm boys, most of them were, who had taken up with the soldiers because they had little choice. And now it was too late. They were as guilty as their leaders. The blood of their countrymen was smeared on their hands.

If the conscripts were hesitant, the officers were not. They were brutal and glaring and arrogant men. Indoctrinated into a cause that was bigger than them, historic, compelling, more important than life, they were focused on the moment and completing the task that *The Brother* had assigned them to accomplish that day.

The senior officer, a captain, stood to the side, swatting casually at flies as he smoked a thin cigarette. He was a squat man, with a thick neck and well-muscled thighs. His dark hair was combed over, hiding the shiny top of his head, and his eyes were black and tightly spaced over his nose. His nostrils flared as he breathed, and his look was intent. He looked to be mid-forty, but his ID revealed he was ten years younger than that.

The captain wouldn't call his job pleasant, but there were worse things to do. And what he did was important. There were subversives in the jungle—sympathizers, former government officials, doctors, lawyers, teachers, and such—and it was his task to find them, to ferret them out, to destroy the subculture where subversives could live. Whether such traitors actually lived in the jungle didn't matter to him. Better to keep hoeing the soil than allow the weeds to take root.

The captain stuffed his hands into his front pockets, then took a deep breath and wet his dry lips. He barked out an order. "The remaining women and children—gather them over here!"

His men jumped at his voice, quickly stepping over the bodies of those who had already been murdered as they herded the villagers toward a clearing in the trees. The officer studied the group of women and children. The adult women were all old; the young and healthy ones having already been taken away. The few children that remained cowered at the back of the crowd, and the women gathered around them like old mother hens. The officer smiled at the sight. His training on the communal farms had proven useful indeed. Breed them, cull them, use them for labor, pelts, or meat. There wasn't much to it. Any fool could succeed.

As he stared at the crowd, a young child caught his eye. She was a beautiful girl with wide, sullen eyes. She looked directly at the captain with a defiant look. The captain approached her and slowly reached out his hand. She recoiled and spat, and the officer laughed. Turning, he moved to the opposite end of the clearing.

The village's twenty-three men were waiting on their knees, positioned shoulder to shoulder. Their heads bent to their chest, for casting their eyes on the officer was a capital crime. The captain walked the line, then grabbed an old man by the hair. Pulling, he forced him to lift his face. "Village leader!" he demanded. The villager hesitated a moment, then glanced down the line, answering the question with a flicker of his eyes.

The captain let go of the old man and strolled down the line. He approached a husky male, stopped, and looked down. "Village leader?" he asked.

The young man nodded slowly.

"Stand."

The man pushed himself up, rising stiffly to his feet. Though he kept his head low, he stuck out his chest. The captain smiled. He liked that. Pride. Confidence. Strutting in the ugly face of death. He could relate to such a man. Perhaps he would let him live.

"Village leader," he asked, "do you know why we are here?"

Of course the man knew. The soldiers were there to steal their food, their wives and young men, to sort out the undesirables—those who could reason, read, or think. The soldiers were there to bring terror. There was no purpose beyond that.

The village leader knew exactly why the soldiers were there. But still he shook his head and answered, "Brother, I don't know."

The officer leaned toward the peasant, smelling the dryness of his breath, a telltale sign of the fear building inside the man's chest. "Yesterday, there were some enemy soldiers on the river," he said. "My spies saw them take out from the river just north of here and move toward your village. Did you see any of these soldiers?"

"Sir, I saw nothing."

"You must have seen something. Why do you lie?"

The man shook his head in terror. "No, sir. No enemy soldiers were here."

The captain took a step back. "Do you think I'm a fool? The enemy soldiers took out of the river just north of here. Where else would they be going? Why do you lie?"

The villager lifted his eyes. "Sir, I swear . . ."

The captain swung violently, striking the villager on the side of his head. "Don't lift your eyes to *me,* pig!" he cried in rage.

The villager forced his head to his chest, the skin on his neck folding into tight rings under his chin. The officer stepped to the side, clearing a visual path between the terrified man and the group of huddled women and children. "Village leader," he asked, "do you have family in this crowd?"

The man shuddered visibly, his shoulders slumping. He looked across the clearing toward the huddled group from his village, quickly glancing into the terrified eyes of his six-year-old girl. She cowered, seeking refuge behind the wall of human flesh. The child caught his eyes, and the man turned away. He then saw his mother, a stooped and broken old woman near the edge of the crowd. She stood away from her grandchild, something they had all learned to do. Families never acknowledged each other when the soldiers were around, for they had learned that the officers liked to kill them in family groups. More efficient. Greater impact. It had all been carefully explained.

The village leader turned his eyes away from his daughter and answered. "I have no family, Captain, but the Great Leader We Love. The Party is my only family, Ankor my only home. There is no family in this village but Brother Number One."

The captain snorted. This man had learned his lessons well.

"That is right, Comrade. Only Brother Number One. Now tell me again—what aid do you provide to the enemy insurgents?"

The village leader lifted his eyes, knowing it mattered not what he said. The officer had made his decision and his fate was now sealed. He knew from experience, from watching others die, that there was nothing he could say now that would change the outcome. Yet he felt almost calm, and a blanket of peace settled over him. He looked at the captain, staring him in the eyes. "I swear to you, sir, I haven't done anything."

The captain studied the man, surprised at his soft tone. So there was no fight left inside him. The captain was disappointed somehow.

The officer turned abruptly and screamed to his sergeants, "Tie this traitor to the tree! We will see if he lies!"

Four of the conscripts came forward and pulled the young father by the arms, dragging him through the wet mud as he struggled to stand. Lifting him by the neck, they threw him against the nearest tree. The groups of villagers were quiet as the man was tied and bound to the tree.

There was no trial, no words, not even a condemnation of death, nothing to mark the decision that had already been made. The captain walked to the canvas-topped army truck that had carried him to the village. Reaching behind the front seat, he pulled out a large leather flask. He had come prepared for something new, something different today. The liquid sloshed in the flask as he approached the condemned man. Pulling the soft cork, he doused the villager with diesel fuel. After soaking the man's hair, head, shirt, and trousers, the captain poured the last cup of fuel on the villager's bare feet.

A young lieutenant came forward, his rifle in hand. "What

are you going to do, Captain?" the lieutenant hissed under his breath.

The officer didn't answer. Wasn't it obvious?

The lieutenant lifted his hand. "There is no need for this. This man hasn't done anything."

The captain motioned to the dead villagers. "Neither did any of these."

The lieutenant glanced at the terrified crowd. "We have done enough here, Comrade Captain. Let's move on up the river now."

The captain reached into his trousers' pocket. "Step aside, lieutenant, or you will find yourself also tied to the tree."

The captain pulled out a small box of matches, then heard a faint cry of despair. Turning, he saw the wide-eyed little girl that had caught his attention before. She was beautiful, yes. A perfect specimen. She should be kept, for she would produce good stock for the Party one day. She looked to be five, maybe six—certainly old enough to understand what was going on. He smiled at her again, cocking his head to the side.

"Your father?" he mouthed to her.

The child stared, eyes wide in fear, then nodded her head.

The captain extracted a match from the box and struck it against the metal sheath that was strapped to his thigh. The wooden match sizzled to life. He let it burn a moment, staring at the flame, then looked at the girl and dropped the match at her father's feet.

The fuel was slow to catch, for the diesel had mixed with the water on the ground and had soaked into the mud. Several seconds passed with no indication of fire. Then a thin stream of black smoke began to issue from the ground. A yellow flame began to flicker, quickly catching at the man's clothes.

The child screamed, and an old woman cried from the back of the crowd. The condemned man took a deep breath and turned away from his family. The flames caught at his trousers, then the tail of his shirt. Deep yellow, almost orange, the flames began to lick higher. Every eye, every head, was turned to the fire. Smoke began to waft through the low trees.

The man cried out in anguish as the little girl bolted from the crowd, running desperately to her father. A conscript stepped forward, but the girl slipped through his grasp, tears streaming down her face as she ran to the tree. She tripped on a low stump and fell at her father's feet. "No, Father! No! You promised you would not leave me!" she sobbed.

The fire grew higher, and she was forced back from the heat. The flames cracked and burned, reaching ten feet into the sky. She reached again for her father, leaning into the heat. "I want to come with you!" she cried. "Don't leave me, Father. Please, I want to be with you."

The man looked down, then closed his eyes for the last time. The officer watched, a satisfied smirk on his face. The fire reached an apex, burning with a bright yellow flame.

The little girl rolled onto her back, swallowing the sickness inside. The captain looked down and their eyes met briefly again. She lay there, unmoving, tears brimming her eyes, then moaned once in anguish and curled into a tight, little ball. She pulled at her knees and her eyes slowly closed. Her breath became heavy, as if she were asleep.

* * *

The vision passed abruptly, and Luke found himself on the floor, his heart pounding inside him, a slamming ache in his chest.

Lucifer stood over him, a somber look on his face.

"Is that how it will be?" Luke cried in anguish, a terrified look in his eyes.

"More or less," the great Deceiver replied. "I can't see the details, and so I fill in the blanks. The exact location and time, other parties in the scene, the landscape and such things, these are hazy to me; but yes, I have shown you the essence of what her mortal life will be."

Luke moaned with a sickness that reached to the pit of his soul. He cried out in anguish. Not his sister, Beth! He swallowed and sat up. He didn't know what to do. "Does it have to be that way?" he groaned in a low voice.

"According to Him, yes, it does."

"But who will cause all that suffering?"

"I don't know," Satan lied. "All I can tell you is it's a part of the plan." *Part of my plan,* Satan laughed in delight to himself. "But remember, dear Luke," he continued, "Jehovah will be the king of the earth. And who else but the king could allow such a thing to take place?"

It was a terrible lie, he knew, but Lucifer didn't skip a beat, for lying now came more easily than telling the truth. And in all of his practice, he had learned a useful trick: the more outrageous the lie, the more likely it was to be believed. *Christ is the deceiver. He doesn't care about you! He won't die for you, but I will! And I don't want his glory. I will share it with you!* His lies grew more and more bold every day, and yet he had never reached a point where he was not believed.

"And remember, Luke," he continued in a dark, gloomy tone, "what I showed you is just a glimpse at the future. There will be so much suffering, you can't even comprehend it."

Luke moaned in anguish. What was he to do? Had he seen a shadow of the truth or just a whisper of lies? He loved Beth! Was there no other way?

"Is that what you want for your sister?" Lucifer taunted as he stood over Luke. "Can you see now we must fight him? Do you have any choice? Will you fight for your sister? Have you the courage to join with us now?"

chapter sixteen

Luke spent that night in the Great Chamber, an honored guest of the Deceiver. Early the next morning, he was introduced to some of Lucifer's most trusted lieutenants. Balaam watched from a dark corner as Luke was escorted down the Great Hallway, ready to start a new life with his friends.

After Luke had passed, Balaam took a deep breath, gathered his courage, and went again to his Master. "I have done what you asked," he said in a quiet voice. "And sir, I would also remind you that I am a man of great stature and esteem in this world. I am a gifted orator, respected by my peers. . . ."

The Deceiver peered toward him, an incredulous look on his face. What was this? Was he hearing things? Could Balaam be such a fool?

"And sir," Balaam continued, missing the significance of Lucifer's disbelieving stare, "you promised that if I convinced Luke to come, you would reward my success. You said that you were going to need men like me to stand at your side, to share the combinations that are so precious to you, the secret oaths and oblations that bring you such power. And remember,

Great Master, Samuel was also my prize. There have been many others. My stable is constantly full. So, given these facts, haven't I earned a reward?"

Lucifer's eyes began to narrow as his lips spread, pulling into an ugly frown that exposed his front teeth. "What are you saying?" he demanded in a menacing tone.

"I'm saying, Master Mahan, that you and I had a deal."

"Then I must have been lying. Now leave me alone."

Balaam didn't move, though his eyes burned with rage. "But you said, my dear Master . . . "

"I know what I said. But I was lying to you. Now go! I am busy. I have other men to deceive."

"You will not honor our agreement?"

"I don't honor *anything!* And I owe nothing to you. I lie. I deceive. Everyone does. It's the way we operate; it's the way things get done. Are you so naïve as to believe I would actually share my power? And my secret oaths and combinations are reserved for mortal men, men who would sacrifice their salvation for power and fame. Now get out of here, Balaam. I want you out of my sight."

"But sir . . . "

"Leave!" Lucifer shouted, his eyes beginning to bulge. He wouldn't be questioned, not by this parasite! His hands began to quiver as he pointed to the great door.

"But Master Mahan, you promised . . . "

Lucifer jumped toward him, a terrible look in his eyes. The room seemed to darken as he lifted his hand. He transfigured in an instant and Balaam stepped back in terror as Lucifer took on the form of a bloody pig's head. The vision hovered before him, right in front of his face—narrow eyes, frothing snout, pink lips, and white tongue. "LEAVE ME!" the pig screamed at the top of his voice. "LEAVE ME, BALAAM, FOR I WON'T SUFFER FOOLS. YOU FORGET, BALAAM,

THAT I AM THE KING OF THIS WORLD! I AM NOT BOUND BY YOUR BARGAINS, AND I DON'T TELL THE TRUTH.

"NOW GO! DEPART FROM ME, OR I WILL HAVE YOU DESTROYED!"

Balaam whimpered in terror as he crawled on all fours from the room. The pig's head hovered behind him, snapping viciously at his heels. Bloody froth dripped below it, staining Balaam's beautiful robe. He whimpered and cried as he crawled from the room.

Entering the Great Corridor, Balaam found himself alone. He glanced behind him in terror, but the pig's head was gone. He stumbled on weak knees to the corner and collapsed on the floor, crying in disappointment and frustration and fear.

* * *

As the night came on, Lucifer brewed alone on his throne. Something wasn't right, he felt unease in his soul, and his evil instincts were screaming, making him feel fidgety and mean. He stood up and cursed, then paced back and forth. Finally, he called to one of his guards.

"Go to the older brother," he commanded.

The guard hesitated. "Samuel?" he asked.

"Yes, of course Samuel. Go to him, make him pack, and get him out of here. He is too close to his brother, and I don't want Luke to see him right now. Neither one of these men is firmly on our side, and if they talk to each other, I can't predict what they'll say. Sam is too unpredictable—he has no allegiance to me. And Luke is uncertain; even he doesn't know what he'll do. It would be much better to keep them isolated and away from each other for now. So go to Sam and get him out of here before the coming day."

* * *

Later that night, the soldier walked into Sam's room without knocking on the door. It was a cramped and dingy apartment with no windows, little furniture, and black paint on the walls. The soldier stepped into the dark chamber, a large bag in his hand.

"You've got to leave," he said as he tossed the bag in Sam's lap. "Pack your things. And hurry. He wants you out of here."

Samuel pushed himself up. "You treat me like a prisoner and I'm tired of it. There's no reason for you to treat me this way."

The soldier glared at him angrily. "Yeah, well, I have my orders. That's all I know."

"I've shown you no reason to doubt me."

"Sometimes the truth doesn't show. And the Master doesn't trust you; that much is pretty clear. He said I need to keep you close, watch and monitor what you do. And like I said, buddy, I just do what I'm told."

Sam glanced down at the roughly sewn bag that had fallen to his feet. "Where are we going?" he asked.

"Somewhere far away. The Master wants you out of here by morning. Now quick, pack your things."

It didn't take long. Then Sam was given instructions on where he should go. He set out on the road, walking alone in the dark.

* * *

As Samuel was packing his bag, far away to the west, Elizabeth looked up at Ammon with tears in her eyes, then back down at the note she held in her trembling hands. She struggled to speak, but the words wouldn't come. Never in her life had she felt such a soul-piercing pain. It cut her so deeply she wondered how she could survive. Sam, her big brother—he had always been so strong. And now Luke. Oh, her Luke! When would this end?

"He's gone!" she cried numbly.

Ammon nodded his head.

"He's gone," she repeated.

Ammon stared at the floor.

chapter seventeen

What do we do, Ammon?" Elizabeth begged, looking desperately for answers.

Ammon thought in silence for a long time, then finally lifted his head. "I'll tell you what we're going to do," he answered. He pushed himself up and moved toward Elizabeth, his eyes no longer defeated but determined and angry. The fighter had risen inside him, and he was ready to move. His back was tight, his shoulders square, his face animated and intense. "First thing," he said, "we're not going to sit here and feel sorry for ourselves. We've done that already and it doesn't change anything. And we're not going to sit around and feel sorry for our brothers, simply praying that one day they'll have a sudden change of heart. It's time to do something. We're going after them. And something else, Beth, we're not going to be scared anymore." He pointed angrily east, toward the Great Liar's cities. "I'm tired of being frightened. I think it's time *he* was afraid of what *we* will do for a change!"

Elizabeth moved toward him and brushed her hands across her face. "But Ammon, how will we find them? Out of billions of people, how will we know where to look? They could be anywhere! And we've already seen that if they don't want us to find them, it is impossible."

"We'll search every house if we have to," Ammon answered. "We'll knock on every door, stand on every street corner and ask everyone we meet. We'll walk every alley, search every square, go to every city. I don't care how long it takes. I don't care if we are uncomfortable or made to feel like fools. I don't care what we sacrifice; none of that matters now. The only thing that matters is our brothers. and we won't stop until we find them. I promise you that."

"But even if we find them, there are no guarantees they'll come back to our side."

"True, we can't make them. But this much I can guarantee. We'll force them to make a final decision while looking us in the eye. No more slipping away in the night, no more leaving without having the courage to tell us good-bye, no more secret notes or hiding behind a wall of new friends. We're going to make them choose: Jehovah or Lucifer, their family or their friends, those who want their happiness or those who want them for pawns in their war. They have to choose either the plan of salvation or destruction, it's as simple as that.

"And if they choose the other, then at least we will know. And we can walk away knowing we are clean of the stain of their sins."

Elizabeth's eyes flashed with a new light. She brushed her hair back, pushing it behind her ear, revealing completely the determined look on her face. There was no more confusion or doubt in her eyes. Ammon instantly recognized the look, and he knew there was no stopping her now. "If we can just find them," she said. "Luke is so tenderhearted, he just got carried away, and there has to be more to Sam's story than we know about. I just have this feeling . . . if we can only find them."

"Okay, then, let's go," Ammon said as he moved for the door. "We need to find someone who can help us. And I think I know where to start."

"Master Balaam?" Beth questioned, her voice suddenly tense.

Ammon slowed and turned, his face flashing with anger. "Never Master Balaam! He's the enemy now. He is as evil and corrupt as any man I have seen."

"I know that," Beth replied. "But still he might be able to help us."

"I would never trust him."

"I'm not suggesting we trust him. I haven't trusted him for some time now. But we don't have to trust him to *use* him, you know."

Ammon was silent, his mouth frozen in surprise. Was this his little sister? Proposing a conspiracy? Ammon almost laughed. "Are you suggesting . . . "

"I'm suggesting that Master Balaam is a proud man. And if we can find him, if we are careful, we might use that pride."

Ammon thought a long moment. "You are clever, Beth, and I love how you think. But we can't go to Balaam. He is poison to us now."

Beth started to argue, but stopped and instead reached for Ammon's hand. "That's fine. But we *are* going to find them. And we *will* bring them back. I can feel it, Ammon. I feel it here in my soul. We are going to find them, even if we have to do this alone."

Ammon placed his hand upon hers and pressed his lips together. "But there is someone who might help us," he offered again.

She looked at him skeptically.

"Teancum," he answered before she had time to ask. "He's like a little fox, sneaking around here and there. He seems to have his own rules in the fight for the cause. And from what I hear . . . well, let's just say he might know where to start."

"Teancum!" Beth cried, clapping her hands to her cheeks. "Oh no, I forgot! Since we found out about Luke, it completely slipped my mind."

"What?" Ammon demanded as his heart skipped a beat.

Elizabeth looked down, embarrassed. How could she forget? But since finding the note from Luke, she hadn't thought of anything else. Ammon moved toward her, reading the look in her eyes. She looked up and told him, "Teancum came here this morning. He was looking for you."

* * *

Teancum pulled the door back and stood in the doorway, his enormous frame filling the empty space, his golden hair shining even in the dim evening light. He didn't move for a moment as he summed the two young people up. "Hello," he said in greeting. That was it, nothing more.

Ammon glanced at Beth. "We'd like to talk to you," he said.

Teancum nodded and answered. "I thought you would be here earlier." Beth looked embarrassed. "Did you tell him?" Teancum asked.

"I didn't remember until a few minutes ago."

"We need your help," Ammon cut in. "We have a brother, two brothers . . . they are gone . . . "

"Yeah, I'm very sorry. I heard about Luke not long ago."

Ammon paused, uncomfortable, then stared at his hands. He thought of the dream, and what Michael had said. He thought of the white school, the pink sweater, and the anonymous boy. Michael had given him a warning, and still he had failed. Inside he was churning, almost sickened from grief. He'd been warned about Luke, and still he had failed.

But it wasn't too late. He would fight for him now.

Ammon thought a long moment, and Teancum watched him carefully. The silence grew uncomfortable until Elizabeth stepped forward and said, "We've heard you might be able to help us. We've heard you've been, you know, over there . . . "

Teancum flashed a quick smile. "Oh, yeah, I've been there. I've scaled their walls and slinked around in the dark. I've listened to their conversations and talked to their guards. I've been inside his new fortress, right there under his nose, right there in his chamber and the Great Hall. And let me tell you," he laughed, clearly proud of himself, "that ol' boy isn't as bright as people make him out to be. He gets a little sloppy, a little too full of himself." Teancum laughed again and then stopped suddenly. "Well, that's probably enough," he mumbled, suddenly sheepish. "Let's just say that you're right. I know a little bit of their city, maybe more than anyone."

Ammon nodded with excitement. "We are going to find our brothers," he said.

Teancum cocked his head knowingly. "I suspected you would."

"Do you think you can help us?"

"I can't go with you, if that's what you mean."

"That's not what we're asking."

"Then what do you want?"

"We need to know where to look. We need to know about their cities, and where we should start. I've been there too, but I only scratched the surface. It sounds like you've gone pretty deep."

Teancum reached out and pulled them inside. "Come on in," he said quickly. "I have to show you something. It's almost over now, and it's time you knew."

They sat around a small table. A smoky fire burned in the fireplace, and the room smelled of apples and pine. It was an old stone and wood house, with ancient beams on the ceilings, dark wooden floors, and a row of tall windows that looked out on a grassy orchard, the trees casting shadows in the nearly full moon. "Tell me about Luke," Teancum said as the three young people sat down.

Beth explained quickly.

"So he left sometime last night?"

"As far as we can tell. But I didn't find the note until this afternoon."

"You realize if you were to ask Michael, he would forbid you to go. He would say you're too young and it's too dangerous now."

Ammon didn't answer. It wasn't what he wanted to hear. "But you have been there," he answered. "And I have too. And we returned safely."

"Not since the last council. He has grown in such power, it isn't safe anymore. Things are happening very quickly, all of the buildup is ready to break. And there isn't any reason to cross the battle lines now. The enemy has become so entrenched in his bitterness and hate that little good comes from talking to them anymore. Our missionaries, all our agents, have been ordered home." Teancum paused suddenly, a knowing look in his eyes. Ammon didn't catch it, but Elizabeth did. "The end will come soon," he concluded. "They are ripe to be destroyed."

Ammon pushed back his hair, then folded his arms. "But you still cross the lines, don't you, Teancum?" he prodded.

Teancum hesitated. "There are some things we still need to know," he replied.

"So you do then?"

Teancum didn't answer, and so Ammon knew. "Have you been over recently?" he pressed.

"Pretty recent, I guess."

"How long ago now?"

Teancum leaned back and rolled his fingers on the table. "Oh, I don't know, let's see, it was . . . last night, I guess." Elizabeth's eyes opened in wonder and she took a deep breath. Teancum glanced toward her and smiled with pride. Ammon didn't react, for he wasn't surprised. Leaning forward, he asked, "Did Michael know you were going?"

"Of course he did."

"You work directly for Michael?"

"I am one of his lieutenants."

"You are always with him. You attend the great councils."

"There is much that I know, if that's what you are getting at."

Beth's eyes burned with excitement. "Then will you help us, Teancum?" she asked. "Please, will you help us find our brothers? We don't know where to go. We don't know where to start."

Teancum was silent for a very long time. He looked at the door, as if waiting, then dropped his eyes to the floor. He tapped his foot impatiently. "There are so many people," he answered. "Billions have now joined him. And if your brother doesn't want you to find him, it will be impossible. And even if I were to tell you where to start, that would not be enough. You're still going to need someone who knows their cities even more than I do."

"We understand that," Beth answered, "But please, Teancum!" Her eyes bore into his soul. "Please, if there is anything, anything at all you could do."

Teancum met her eyes, then looked across the table to Ammon. "She's your little sister?" he asked.

"Yes, Teancum."

"She can be pretty persuasive."

"Believe me, I know."

Teancum glanced impatiently toward the door, then stood and began to pace around the room. "Okay, then," he said, slapping the table as he stood. "I agree, we've got to find Luke. He hasn't been there very long, so it won't be as difficult, but you're still going to have to act quickly, before they can move him around . . . "

Ammon raised his hand suddenly. "Why do you keep saying that?" he interrupted.

"Saying what?" Teancum asked him.

"You keep referring to *him*. It's *them*, our two brothers. You know there are two."

Teancum almost smiled, then sat down again. "Oh, well," he sighed. "It would have been much more exciting to show you, but I guess I have run out of time."

"Show us what?" Beth questioned.

"Remember I said there was something that you need to know? I was hoping I could show you, but we don't have any more time. If we are going to find Luke, we are going to have to act . . . "

There came a sudden knock on the door. Teancum jumped up, excited, his eyes bright and alive. "Finally!" he cried as he ran to the entryway. He glanced back at his friends, then pointed to the door. "This is so great!" he laughed, a huge smile on his face. "I mean it! This is great . . . no, this is better than that . . . !"

The knock sounded again and he winked, then pulled the door back.

Elizabeth cried. Ammon gasped.

And Sam stepped into the room.

chapter eighteen

Every eye fell on Sam as he walked into the cramped room. Time came to a stop, and the heavens stood still. The air seemed to crackle, and the only sound that could be heard was Elizabeth's heavy breath, then a cry that she tried to hold in her chest. Sam walked into the room, slowly, deliberately, almost cautiously, a sheepish look on his face. His clothes were dirty and worn, and his bare feet were covered with dust, but his dark hair was pushed back and his smile was as bright as ever. He looked beaten, very tired, but his face almost glowed. He moved to the center of the room and came to a stop, turning to Teancum, then Ammon, then Beth. She sat there, dumbfounded, with trembling hands. "Sam," she almost whispered, her eyes wide and bright. "Sam," she repeated, struggling to hold in a sob.

He nodded and smiled, then lifted his hands. She gasped and jumped up, knocking her chair to the floor, hesitated a moment, then ran into his arms. "Sam!" she repeated again and again. "Sam! Sam! I can't believe it is you!"

"I love you," he whispered.

"I know you do, Sam. Despite everything, I always knew."

Samuel lifted his head and looked toward his younger brother. Ammon hesitated, unbelieving, then pushed himself up and moved toward them. Turning, Elizabeth wiped the tears from her eyes. The three siblings looked at each other, then embraced for a very long time.

The young men finally sat at Teancum's white table. Beth didn't sit, but stood at Ammon's side, her hand on his shoulder, leaning on him for support. Sam placed his arms on the table and leaned forward, staring at his hands, waiting for the questioning to begin. Ammon stared at his brother. "Sam," he finally said, "What . . . ? Why . . . ?" He didn't know where to start.

Sam looked up, his face serious. "This won't be easy to explain."

Beth lifted a finger and played anxiously with her hair. "Sam, where have you been?"

Sam looked away as he searched for the words. Teancum shot up, pushing away from the table. "I'll tell you where he's been," he said in a loud voice. "You are looking at a hero." He jabbed a hand toward Sam. "You are looking at a man who was willing to sacrifice anything—his freedom, his comforts, even the family he loved—all for the Father and the work of his Son. He is a hero and he deserves nothing but our respect and praise."

Sam looked away awkwardly as he shook his head. "I don't deserve anything," he started to say.

"Yes, you do!" Teancum shouted, his hands flailing the air to emphasize his point. "Do you realize," he said, turning to Ammon and Beth, "that Sam volunteered for a mission, a treacherous and demanding task? It was dirty, depressing, and lonely, and he was all the time on his own, cut off entirely from his family. Even those of us who knew, we couldn't do anything. It was impossible for us to help him.

He had to work on his own. This is a real hero here!" Teancum paused and lowered his voice. "There are so many you have helped," he said as he turned to Sam. "James and Tia and Raquel. Paul and his brothers. There are so many you identified and led to the light—hundreds, maybe more, owe their salvation to you. You went into the darkness to search these people out. You took on the burden of living in their dark world. You saw those who had goodness, even a flicker of light. You were the key, the beginning of bringing them home. And they are so thankful. There's not enough I can say."

Teancum fell suddenly quiet, then sat down again. His blond hair fell back and he pushed it away. "I tell you," he said with a voice of admiration. "You . . . all of you," he looked at the three, "you are one special family. I can see it so clearly. I'm honored to call you my friends."

Ammon stared at Teancum, still not able to comprehend, then turned to his brother, an amazed look on his face. "Sam, will you tell us what Teancum is talking about?"

"It's not easy to explain."

"Then get going," Ammon said.

Teancum glared at Sam. "Come on, Sam!" he coaxed. "You don't have to be humble." He thumped his chest and smiled. "You and me, we are warriors! We're the peacocks in the garden, so go on, strut a bit." Ammon watched him and laughed, knowing he was being sarcastic but knowing also that was how Teancum really felt.

Samuel glanced at the window. "I'd rather talk about Luke. He is all that matters now."

"No, Sam," Elizabeth answered. "We need to know about you first. We can't go after Luke until morning anyway. Now please, will you tell us what is going on?"

Sam took a long breath. "It all started," he offered,

"quite a long time ago. Right after the Great Council, when Jehovah and Lucifer presented their views about the plan of salvation, when the lines between forces began to form. As you know, all of my closest friends . . . " Sam turned away, then continued, his voice suddenly sad, "every single one of my friends, all of those people I loved, for reasons I don't understand, they all chose to follow Lucifer. They tried to get me to follow him also, but there was no way I would go. Over time, some of them became leaders in Lucifer's army. As his followers began to separate themselves from the children of God, as they moved to other cities and began to congregate together, they became more and more bitter and began to lose their freedoms and ability to operate on their own. As a result, it became more and more difficult to send missionaries among them. But we knew there were some among Lucifer's people for whom there was still hope. But time was getting short, and it was difficult, even dangerous, to work in the cities over which Lucifer had control. Our missionaries were outnumbered, and they were constantly harassed. But there were a few, just a few, who still had the light of Christ in their souls.

"So Michael came to me and asked me if I would volunteer to go among Lucifer's followers, secretly, quietly, not bringing attention to myself, and talk to them, live with them, identify those who were not so calloused and angry, those who might change their minds, those who had secret doubts about Lucifer's way."

Ammon shook his head in amazement. It was entirely new, a concept so foreign it had never entered his mind. "You mean," he slowly mumbled, "Michael asked you to volunteer to live on their side, to help him identify who might still be saved?"

"Yeah," Samuel answered. The sheepish smile returned.

"Pretty amazing, isn't it. I mean, who would have suspected? And the great thing is, it actually worked. I was able to identify so many children—where they lived, who they were, what they were feeling inside—and send their names to Michael, who would send missionaries to them."

Sam finished speaking and reached into his clothes. Pulling out a folded piece of paper, he shoved it into Teancum's hand. "My last list," he proclaimed. "There are only seven names there. And they won't be easy, for it would appear that the day of harvest has passed. But if Michael chooses, it might be worth one more try to send someone to make final contact with them."

"There is so little time left," Teancum answered sadly as he took the folded note.

"Yes, I know. I did what I could before I had to come home." Samuel sat back in silence. "And now my mission is complete."

"But, Sam," Elizabeth asked in a quiet voice, "why didn't you tell us? Why couldn't we know?" Her face was soft with hurt, her eyes narrow with rejection and pain.

Samuel lowered his head. "I'm sorry," he answered in a deep, weary voice. "Michael wanted me to tell you. But I was afraid."

"I don't understand," Beth replied as she wiped a tear from her eye.

Sam was quiet a moment. "Let me ask you something," he finally said. "If you had known what I was doing, and Balaam had come to you, would you have been able to deceive him? Would you have been able to lie?" He glanced toward Ammon. "The same question to you."

Neither one of them answered. "And that's why I couldn't tell you," Sam replied. "Neither one of you is capable of telling a lie. And even if you had found a way not to answer, Balaam still would have known. The first time he talked to you, he would have known something was wrong. He has an incredible power of perception and though his gift is fading now, still he would have known. He would have seen it in your eyes and heard it in your voice. And if he knew of my mission, I would have been forced to come home immediately.

"I'm very sorry," Sam concluded. "But I didn't realize at first I would be gone so long. And it was working so well. We were finding so many souls, I got caught up in the work. I knew it would hurt you, but I didn't know what else to do. Perhaps it wasn't perfect, maybe there was another way, but I only wanted to help . . . " His words trailed off.

The room grew silent as Sam's voice fell against the wooden walls. "I hope you can forgive me," he muttered finally.

Elizabeth moved around the table and leaned her head on his shoulder. "I'm so proud of you," she answered as she put her arms around him. Sam reached for her hand, then glanced over to Ammon.

"You have always been my hero," Ammon answered proudly. "And you are even more now."

Teancum watched them a moment, then slapped his hand on the table again. "All right!" he concluded. "I'm glad we got that settled. Now let's talk about Luke."

Sam focused on Ammon, his face drawing tight. "You've got to go find him," he said. "I can tell you where they have him, but I can't go there with you."

"You've got to go," Elizabeth said, shifting her eyes toward Ammon. "You might be the only one he will listen to now."

"And you're going to have to hurry," Samuel cut in urgently. "And know this, my brother, there will be a personal assault. Satan will be waiting to deceive you and throw roadblocks in your way. He will not let you get close to Luke without paying a price. He will come after you, Ammon, and he is *so* powerful, he has powers of both persuasion and fear that are hard to believe. He has studied all of us for such a long time that he knows all of our weaknesses right down to the core, and he will tailor his words to test your very soul."

The room fell silent again, the air heavy and still.

"Ammon will make it," Elizabeth answered as she turned to Sam. "Lucifer may be powerful, but I have complete faith in our brother."

chapter nineteen

The black and gray clouds seemed to hold the hot air against the ground, forming a blanket of oppressive heat that clung to the mountains. Even the low-lying valleys couldn't catch a fresh breath. Behind him, Ammon heard the thunder rumble again, the sound echoing off the mountains and rolling along the valley floor. The thunder was brutal and angry, as if it were the utterance of a curse, a violent expression of fury and storm. The dark clouds began rolling into swirling pools of black, and he felt a great gust of wind and the air turn suddenly cold. An enormous drop of rain, single and fat, fell on the dusty road right in front of his feet and formed into a tiny ball of dirt that was quickly absorbed. Ammon waited, then turned to see the coming storm. The air turned gray and then black as the wall of water approached. Another drop hit his face. Lightning flashed, thunder rolled, and the rains came pounding down. The wall of water hit him, driven by biting wind. He was instantly soaked, sending a chill to his very core.

He put his back to the storm and continued walking along the road. Lucifer's city sat up high on the hill. It loomed in shadows; despite the rain and deep overcast, few lights were burning there. The road leading into the capital became crowded as he neared the outer wall.

Drawing closer, he could see that the streets teamed with people, all of them cursing and pushing, accusing their friends, hoarding supplies, tugging at each other and crying in fear. It wasn't a riot, but it was very close, with breaking glass, smoking fires, and chaos in the streets. The pouring rain drenched the crowd, seeming to settle them from a frenzy into a dull roar. The filthy streets became mucky, in some places almost ankle deep in mud. Ammon stood outside the city gates until the wall of rain had passed, leaving behind a dull drizzle that splattered dirty raindrops on the muddy ground.

The crowd rushed around him, pushing him here and there. Ammon glanced at the people, seeing the hate and fear in their eyes. What was it, he wondered, that had set them to rage? Then he heard the whispered voices and finally understood.

They had heard the rumors. They were going to be cast out.

Cast out to darkness. Denied the presence of God. Cast down to hell.

No one knew, not for certain anyway, what these words even meant. *Cast out. Hell and darkness.* What did it mean? Yet, despite the confusion, the looming threat from God caused a rising anger in their hearts, a bitterness so thick it hung like a stench in the air. "Who are *you* to cast *us* out?" he heard people curse. "You are not *my* king!! I hate you! I loathe you! Why won't you let us be?"

Ammon stepped back in horror. He felt filthy and violated even to hear the words.

"Who is *he* to come here and tell *us* what to do?" another said. "We worship another! We don't want *him* for our king!"

Ammon felt a sudden sickness. Even in their fear, they were still mocking God. He recoiled at their words, hiding his anger inside. He wanted to fight them, destroy them, have them sent away. But he couldn't. Not now. And it didn't matter anyway.

The day was soon coming, in fact, it was nigh; if not today, then tomorrow, their day of destruction was here.

Ammon stood at the gates, standing off to the side and watching the people rage against the truth. These people knew they were doomed. It was too late for them. They had been in open rebellion, cursing and mocking their God. They had fought against him overtly, seeking to pull him from his throne, seeking to usurp his power and claim it for their own—and if they could not claim his power, then to see him destroyed and to take down as many of his children as they could with them.

The day of repentance was over. The day of destruction was near.

"Cast us out!" Ammon heard an angry woman whisper to her friend, "I don't know what that means, but if it means getting out of his kingdom, then I am for that anyway. I hate it here. I hate them all. Blubbering, self-righteous fools! I want to get as far away from them as I can."

He shuddered when he heard it. It was inconceivable. An *eternity* of darkness. *Unending* misery and woe. There was no way to comprehend it, and he shuddered again. The rain pattered on his forehead and ran cold down his neck. He shivered as he watched, then turned away from the crowd.

He had to find Luke. He had to find him right now.

Walking through the arched opening cut out of the enormous stone wall, Ammon followed the road into the inner city, with its bustling, noisy, and obnoxious crowds. Many eyed him closely, if quickly, as they passed by. It was obvious he was an outsider—he was one of *the enemy*—but they were too occupied with their own destruction to accost him for now.

He stood for a moment at a triple fork in the road. One road wound through the city, toward the central square; a second dropped toward the valley, where row upon row of high-rise houses had been built. A third road, better maintained, but narrow and tightly-curved, ran up toward the mountains until it was lost in trees.

Ammon studied the three roads, thinking of what Samuel had told him, then chose the narrow road and began walking quickly. The road was steep and covered with a canopy of trees. Raindrops ran along the branches and collected on the leaves before falling in huge drops that he could feel through his clothes. A canyon rose up on one side and, though it was only late afternoon, the dark clouds and steep canyon walls combined to block out most of the light. The higher he climbed, the darker it got. After a sharp bend, the road straightened out and opened up from under the enormous trees, and he realized he had climbed out of the canyon and up the side of the mountain. Ahead of him, he saw a great stone castle, dark spires of black granite reaching up toward the afternoon sky. Looking upon it, he gasped, his fury building inside. Though smaller, the castle of Satan was an exact replica of the Great Capitol. Black and imposing, it mocked the design with crooked spires and twisted towers that bent to the east. It had the same windows, painted black, the same grand door, the same stairs, a statement of mean-spirited derision of all that had been left behind.

Ammon studied the dark castle, surrounded by a great wall, then turned, looking down and beyond, following the road with his eyes. The road ran past the castle into a thick grove of trees. Above the trees, he could see the metal roofs of the buildings, a series of apartments where the new people were housed. He turned and quickly made his way down the road. Descending below the castle, the road was swallowed again in the trees, and Ammon felt an enormous sense of relief to be out of sight of the dark windows and black walls.

Continuing along the road, he found the buildings where his brother was housed—identical steel and rock apartments that were tall and dark, with few windows and only one door. They were built so close to the road that the doors swung out on the street. A series of roads spread before him, like the spokes of a wheel. He thought again of Sam's instructions, then chose the third road. Quickening his pace—he was growing anxious now, as a building sense of doom crept into his chest—he walked past the first five dwellings and stopped at the sixth. Stepping back, he looked up at the tall building. It was narrow but deep, and the stone walls were slippery from the rain. The rainwater dribbled down the stone, collecting along the chiseled mortar before running to the muddy street. Ammon took a deep breath, then opened the door.

He faced a dark hallway. There was a door on his left and one on his right. A set of steep stairs wound its way up a dark and narrow stairway. He moved to the stairway and started to climb. The air seemed to grow heavier with each step he took; stale and oppressive, it took his breath away. The stairway was hot, and a shudder ran down his spine. On the second floor, two more doors greeted him. He stopped and looked up. The stairs seemed to go on forever. What kind of illusion was this? He felt so tired, so tired, exhaustion seeping into his bones. Another step, another corner. Come on, Ammon, climb! He bent his head, concentrating on moving his feet. The air grew hotter, more heavy, more oppressive and stale. He looked up again. How many floors to go? He climbed, growing weaker. Sam hadn't warned him of this. He stopped, breathing heavily, then looked up again. Despite the exertion and the oppressive surroundings, inside he felt neither fear nor concern. In fact, he seemed to feel nothing at all. He felt completely blank, like an empty, sandy beach that has been washed smooth by a storm.

He kept his head down. Only one flight to go. One more step, then another, his breathing heavy and slow. Rounding the corner, he looked up again.

And there he was, waiting, an ugly smile on his face. He wore a high-collared tunic over a gray and black robe.

"My brother," he said. "I've been waiting for you."

Ammon recoiled in anger. Inside, he was sick. Had it all been for nothing? Was he already too late? "You are not my brother," he said. "You are nothing to me."

"I've been waiting for you. I know why you are here," Lucifer said, nodding toward a wooden door to his left. "He's inside this room."

Ammon hesitated. "Luke is in there?" he asked.

"Of course he is. Isn't everything just like Samuel said it would be, just like that traitor, that lying and treacherous scum . . . " Lucifer cursed violently, his eyes flashing in yellow rage. He lowered his head quickly, hiding the fury inside, then took a deep breath and lifted his head. "Yes, Luke is here. And he is waiting for you."

Ammon took a single step upward. "Will you let me talk to him now?"

Lucifer lifted his palms in an expression of peace. "How could I stop you? If you want to talk to him, there's not a thing I can do. If he chooses to go with you, that's his decision, not mine. Luke has his agency; all of my followers do. I can't force them to come here, and I can't force them to stay. I only have the power to *persuade* them. I can't *force* anything.

And even if I could, I wouldn't coerce anyone, for I am much better, much stronger when they *want* to stay."

Ammon took another step forward. Only three steps to go. The Deceiver stepped back, moving out of his way. The stairs were very narrow, and Ammon would have to press against him as he passed on the stairs.

Lucifer lifted his hand and pointed again. "Go. Luke is in there," he said.

Ammon took another step; then Lucifer moved back into his way. "Before I let you in," he said softly, "I just wish you would listen to me. I'm begging you, Ammon, for Luke, for Elizabeth, for the sake of the others!"

The shadows seemed to shift as he spoke, casting his face in a different light. Looking at him now, he seemed so incredibly sincere, his face handsome, truthful and kind. Ammon felt almost as if he were talking to an old friend. Satan smiled. "It's only me," he said, dripping with charisma. It was a beautiful show. And though Ammon knew it was showtime, that none of this was real, it was still so inviting, so enticing, so real.

He took a deep breath, wanting to sit down and rest. And while he was resting, he would listen to him. It only seemed fair to hear his point of view.

But he shook his head to clear it. "I've heard it already," he said wearily, mustering as much conviction in his voice as he could. "There is nothing more you could say."

Lucifer stared down, a look of hurt on his face. Then suddenly, almost instantly, he moved down the step next to Ammon, a movement of shadow so quick it was little more than a flicker of light. He brushed up beside him, literally right in his face, his breath hot on his cheek, his black cape swirling around Ammon's knees. "I want to tell you something," he whispered in Ammon's ear. "Listen to me, brother. Listen to what I have to say.

"There is so much I can give you. So much you could have! Imagine untold worlds, galaxies, and stars, and they go on forever, from beginning to end. Imagine worlds and kingdoms, princes and kings, warriors and soldiers, princesses and queens, and all of them, Ammon, will be under your control, worlds without number, power beyond your dreams! Every fantasy, every whim, every lust or ambition, every desire, no matter how grand or depraved—imagine *anything* you could wish for, and I will give it to you! Anything you can dream of, any human or thing, any taste, touch, or feel—all the wealth in the universe, I would share it with you. Imagine every law or power, every theory of fairness or eternal principle, every law or commandment to be at your control! Imagine the power to impose a hundred million slaves at your whim, every wish you conceive of being immediately fulfilled. Come with me, Ammon, and I will give you all this and more. And it will be yours forever. *It will never end!* Come with me, work with me, do what I say, follow my commandments, and I will give this to you! And all I ask is you believe me and do what I say."

Ammon felt his knees quiver at the feel of Lucifer's touch. The Deceiver put his cold arms around him, and Ammon's heart seemed to withdraw in his chest, beating wildly, as if trying to flee. A sudden sensation came over him at the touch of Lucifer's hand, and his mind seemed to open, as if he could see *everything!* Everything he had promised was brought to his eyes. Every glory and power, every sensation and desire—it all lay before him, like a table finely spread, running from his feet to the never-ending stars. The pull was so powerful it drew at his soul, pulling him, drawing him, grabbing his heart. He struggled to withdraw, but he seemed helpless to move.

Yes, he could have it. And why not? Why not now?

He reached out to touch it, but the vision withdrew. "Not yet," Lucifer whispered again in his ear. "You must say the words before I'll give it to you. You must pledge to me, Ammon . . . "

The vision opened again.

Everything he had ever wanted was waiting for him. Ammon closed his eyes and swallowed against the terrible battle inside. His heart raced again, and he wondered if he would survive. He couldn't speak, he couldn't think, and he was overcome with despair. A deep blackness fell upon him, and he thought he might be destroyed. Could he live through this cold touch? Was it over for him?

And he wanted it so, be it right or wrong. He wanted this vision, and he wanted it now. He swallowed again, then slowly opened his eyes.

"You can give me anything?" he asked.

"*Anything!*" Lucifer cried.

"Anything I ask for?"

"*Anything* you desire!"

"Can you give me love?" Ammon asked him. "Can you take away my sins? Can you give me salvation? Are you willing to die for me? Can you give me the love of my family and the love of my friends? Can you promise me anything besides what you have shown me here? Can you give me the love of my Father, or my older brother, Jehovah, the Christ?"

Lucifer stepped back, a look of rage on his face. "Worship me!" he commanded.

Ammon turned away, his legs weak, his arms so heavy they drooped like dead weights at his side. "You have nothing to offer," he said in a quiet voice. "Now get out of my way. I came for my brother Luke."

Lucifer shrieked with such a fury that it pierced Ammon's ears. "Let me show you what I'll give you!" he screamed in a rage. "Let me show you, Ammon, what I've got in store for you!"

Another vision opened, and Ammon gasped in heart-wrenching fear. In an instant he saw all the horrors of the world, all the pain and ambition, all the murders and fraud, the torture, the abuse, the manipulation and lies, the broken families and disappointments, the fatherless children and mothers with empty arms. He saw the blood, death, and horror Lucifer would rain on the earth. He gasped and stepped back, a look of shock and fear in his eyes.

Lucifer watched, then stepped toward him, cursing as he moved. Thrusting a finger, he sneered in Ammon's face. "I will find you," he promised. "I will remember this day. I will find you and curse you when you go down to earth. I will turn every rock and obstacle in your way. If you won't join me in hell, I will bring hell to you. I may not win, but I promise I will make you infinitely miserable. Who knows what I plan? I may curse you with disease, take the lives of your children, or kill others you love. I may arrange a crippling accident to break your precious body in two, make you poor, make you fail, make you depressed and alone, cause you heartbreak and misery. So many things I can do!

"So remember this day, Ammon, and even if you can't, I will remember you. And I curse you now, Ammon, for not following me. But I will get even, I will have the last word. I will create a special hell and bring it to you."

Lucifer sputtered and cursed, then fell silent, his eyes burning like a dying fire on a cold winter night. Then he thrust his face toward Ammon and sneered once again. "I will *never* forget you!" he cried as he cursed.

Ammon stared at him, unflinching. "Perhaps you will do those things," he replied, his voice calm and peaceful, his eyes bright and alive. He took a step toward him, completely unafraid anymore. "Do what you will. I don't fear you now. I understand, can't you see that? I know what you can and can't do to me now.

"You can tempt me, desert me, or cause me great pain; you can create a dark world that may cause me to fear; you can rule your world with blood and terror, that's true.

"But you can't win. And I know that. Weak as I am, with my imperfections and sins, even with all of my failings, I am stronger than you.

"I will soon have a body. And I have my agency now. I will increase in my faith and knowledge and power. I am not perfect, but I will be, and there's not a thing you can do! I will become like the Father if I follow the Son. You are powerless to stop me. You can threaten and tempt and whisper lies in my ear, but you can't stop me, Satan; I see that so clearly now! I can stop myself, yes, but only if I follow you.

"And I reject your temptations. I reject your whispered lies. I reject you, Lucifer, and your entire plan. You have no power to control me. I am in control of myself. And try as you might, you won't control me on earth. We will defeat you in heaven, and we will defeat you on earth. Here, or the earth, it doesn't matter; I am *always* stronger than you."

Ammon stopped and took a breath, squared his shoulders, and smiled.

A sudden chill seemed to sweep from the rafters as Lucifer took a step back. He screamed out in rage, lifting his arms to the skies. He cursed and he ranted, shrieking in frustration and fear, then shook his fist to the heavens and suddenly disappeared.

Ammon stood in the shadows, weak, but without fear. Time passed, but slowly, as he gathered himself. He realized he was crying, his cheeks wet with tears. How long he stood there in the stairway, he didn't know, but after a time he gained strength enough to push himself up the stairs. He lifted one foot, then the other, until he reached the last stair. Turning, he moved toward the wooden door.

Pushing the door open, he stepped into the dark room.

But the small room was empty. And no one was there. He searched frantically, running into the back rooms. The apartment was empty, and there were no windows or doors.

Then he heard the dark laugh from someplace far, far away. "I lied to you," Lucifer screamed, his voice echoing up from below. "I lied to you, Ammon. Your brother isn't there.

"You can't find him. You'll never find him. He is gone! It's too late! You have lost—he is mine now—and there's not a thing you can do. He is angry and bitter and under my control. I have him! He's my angel! And he will be cast out with me. He will be with me, little Ammon; he will be with me on earth. He will be trying to destroy you, along with my other angels of darkness.

"So be ready for us, Ammon! Because we are coming for you."

chapter twenty

Ammon fell to his knees, sick with depression and defeat. He had tried. He had failed. Lucifer had won. Even though they had warned him, he had failed his brother still.

"No!" he cried in frustration and grief. He felt his heart breaking, a tearing pain in his chest. "No, Luke, come back! I love you!" he cried. "Don't go with him, Luke. If you can hear my voice, please come back to me."

But there was no answer, only the darkness and gloom. Deadly silence. Ammon dropped his head to his knees and cried into his hands. "Luke, we were brothers. We were brothers!" he cried.

Then he felt a warm touch on the top of his head. A sudden light filled the darkness, and he felt instantly warm. "I, too, am your brother," he heard his Savior say.

Ammon lifted his head to see Jehovah there. He was kneeling beside him, one arm on his shoulder, one hand on his head. "I, too, am your brother," he repeated again.

A sudden surge of relief chased the pain and darkness away, the dark sense of failure fleeing away from the light. The weight seemed to lift from his shoulders as if it were turned into air. He felt a warm sense of peace, like he was waking from a terrible dream.

"Do you remember my promise?" the Savior asked tenderly.

Ammon couldn't answer for a moment, then sputtered, "Yes, Lord, I do."

"What did I tell you, Ammon?"

"You promised you would not leave me comfortless, that you would come for me."

"Because I am your brother."

"I know, Lord, I know . . . "

"But I am also Luke's brother," the Savior then said.

Ammon buried his face shamefully. "And I know that you love him," he cried miserably. "And I tried to reach him, but I got here too late. And now he is gone. Lucifer claims he is with him. And what now can I do, Lord? I've done all I know how to do. You gave me this responsibility, and I have failed you both."

Jehovah squeezed his shoulder, and Ammon glanced up to see a familiar look in his eyes. "Will you go to him, Lord?" Ammon begged. "Will you talk to him, please."

"I already have," Jehovah answered. "I talked with him last night."

Ammon looked around, dejected. Then why wasn't Luke there? "And what did you say to him, Lord?" he asked quietly.

"We talked about the only things that really matter in life."

Ammon looked confused. He did not understand. He moved over and leaned against the dark wall. His oldest brother knelt beside him and tried to explain. "Listen to me, Ammon," Jehovah began, "everyone—you, Elizabeth, all your brothers and sisters—you have to ask yourselves this question. What is greater inside you, your love or your fear? Do you believe that I love you? Will you trust me enough to follow the Father's plan, despite the uncertainty for the future and the chance you might fail? Will you trust me enough to take a single step into the dark? Do you believe me when I tell you that I will take hold of your hand? Do you love me, Ammon? That is all that matters anymore. Do you love me more than these? Do you love me more than anything else?"

"But you know I love you!"

"Yes, I know that you do. You have proven that, Ammon. And I am so proud of you."

Ammon glanced around the empty room once again. "But what about Luke? If you asked him these questions, tell me, what did he say?"

Jehovah rose up, his face shining warmly. "Why don't I let him tell you?" he said with a smile.

The door slowly opened, and Luke stepped into the room. He took three steps forward, paused, and lowered his head. "I'm so sorry," he said softly as he stared into Ammon's eyes.

"Luke!" Ammon cried, pushing himself to his feet.

"I'm so sorry," Luke repeated.

Ammon ran to his brother, grabbed him by the shoulders and pulled him close to his chest. "It's over now, Luke." he cried in relief.

"Come on," Luke answered. "It's time to go."

chapter twenty-one

Sometime after Lucifer and his angels were cast out of heaven, the physical world was completed and, beginning with Michael, those who had kept their first estate were sent down to earth. A chosen few had been assigned to come later in time, and they continued their training, developing their talents and preparing themselves for the challenge of living in a physical world, a world where Lucifer was now free to roam. Those who had fought Satan in the premortal world, having tasted his temptations and seen the hateful being he had become, having witnessed the jealousy that raged in his angels' souls, understood they would need extraordinary character to protect them on earth.

Not surprisingly, those who had not engaged Lucifer in the war, those who had not fought in the forefront of the battle, those who supported the plan of salvation but were not as valiant in defending it—all these spent far less time preparing for their time on earth. A lesser commitment had carried them to this point, and they saw no reason why it wouldn't be sufficient to carry them through to the end.

But those who fought Satan understood they were wrong. Their time was coming. And the test would be real.

* * *

Like many of the valiant, Ammon and his siblings were withheld from the world until the very last day, until the very last hour, being sent down when Lucifer was at the peak of his power. As the time grew near, Father called them together to give his final instructions and tell them good-bye.

As they approached, the Father smiled and they ran to his side.

"Are you afraid?" he asked Elizabeth, and she nodded her head. He reached out and placed his hand on her cheek. "Passing into the next world isn't like passing through a thin veil. It is more of a dark and long washing, like black water coming down, washing you, immersing you, sending you into the second estate. It's a little bit frightening," he nodded to Beth, "and you are going to feel pain for the very first time. But it won't be anything you can't handle. I have a very deep faith in you."

The siblings were quiet. They would all go down soon—first Sam, and then Ammon, followed by Luke and then Beth.

Luke shot a worried look toward Beth as he thought of the vision he'd seen. "Will it be like Lucifer showed me?" he asked worriedly.

The Father frowned a little. "I'm afraid that it will." He put his arm around Beth. "But you will make it," he assured her. "I know how strong you've become. And remember, all of you, that I will always be there.

"Now come. I want to show you something before you have to go."

As they looked up, they saw the heavens opened, and they beheld the universe, the galaxies and stars, the worlds without number, like the sands of the sea. The creations went on forever, beyond what they could comprehend or endure.

Then they saw one great family working and laughing and playing with God, a sustained march of people that extended from brother Michael to the last child born, one chain, an eternal lineage of brothers and sisters and husbands and wives. And there were children, so many children, young and beautiful. And all of the family, every single individual, looked content and joyful, full of peace and happiness.

Sweeping his arms across eternity, the Father explained, "I am sending you to earth at a very treacherous time. Once you are there, you will forget everything. And the things you will deal with will *seem* so important to you. Your everyday problems will seem incredibly *large*—your work and your school, your family and friends, what to wear, how you look. Are you fat? Are you strong? Are you pretty? Are you smart? Do you make enough money? Do other people like you? Why weren't you chosen for a game or group activity? Why isn't life always fair? Worries such as these may consume you and take all your time.

"You may obsess with disappointments; you may put all your focus on the pain. It will be easy to forget that life is *always* good—that whether you are here or on earth, *you are meant to find joy.*

"So on quiet nights in the summer, when you are still and peaceful, I want you to look up at the heavens, the moon and the stars, so your spirit can remember these things I have shown you today. And if you do, you will remember, somewhere deep in your soul, that you are a part of a heavenly family, a heavenly plan, something eternal and wonderful and incredibly large. You will remember that your family is up here cheering for you, that family is the only thing that matters, the only thing of any significance. And though your human language won't have words for the feelings I will place in your hearts, your spirit will remember and you will long to be with me again."

Beth reached toward her Father, touching him with a trembling hand. "But Father," she pleaded, "how will we know? Everything will be forgotten. Everything we have worked for—all the sacrifice and hope, all the trials and the lessons that brought us to this place—all of it will be forgotten when we pass through the veil.

"So please, won't there be something to remind us of who we used to be? I've seen the world, dear Father, and it's a dark, dangerous place. And if we can't remember that you love us, how are we going to know?"

Father thought a moment as he considered her words. "You are right, Beth," he answered, "the world is a dangerous place. The war with Satan isn't won; it has only changed battlegrounds.

"But if you listen, I will tell you. If you listen closely, you will know. I will whisper to you through father's blessings and a mother's sweet songs. I will talk to you through my prophets and the words they write down. I will give a special blessing to you through a chosen patriarch. And there are other gifts I will send you: bishops, teachers, family members, and friends. I will send my Spirit to guide you. I will not leave you alone.

"And remember, my children," the Father said, looking at all of them, "it doesn't matter so much what you *know,* but it very much matters who you *are!* And who you are isn't left here in this premortal world. The veil over your memories won't change the spirit inside. Who you are doesn't change when you go down to earth, and the sacrifices you have made here will help to carry you through."

The Father stepped back and cast a piercing eye at his

sons. "Now, I have a word of warning to give you," he said solemnly. "Each of you will be blessed with incredible prosperity. You will never lack for freedom or protection or food. You will never go hungry or fear for your lives. You will not suffer overmuch with ill health or live with disease. Instead, you will enjoy every luxury and live a life of great ease.

"But I want you to open your hearts to the fact that there is great suffering in the world, suffering you may not readily care about because it won't be easy to see—little children who are starving, cripples who beg on the street, children who live every day in fear of their lives, malnourished and scared and lonely and cold."

"But Lord, it isn't fair," Ammon cried in distress. "Why will you give us so much while others are left to beg?"

"I ask different things of different children. The challenges I give others I will give for reasons I know. But in the end, there is more parity to the test than will be evident at first."

"Then what will you ask of us, Father?"

"I only ask that you share some of the bounty I give. And when it comes to my kingdom, you have to be willing to give whatever I ask. To a great measure that is how I will judge you when you come back to me."

The siblings looked at each other. It was so little to ask. Then the Father put his arms around them and drew all of them close to him. "I have one more thing to ask you," he said in a loving voice.

"What is it?" Samuel answered. "You know we will do anything."

"Sometime on earth, you will come into contact with each other. How and when that will happen must remain a mystery to you. But when you meet up with each other, the Spirit will speak to your souls, *This is my brother! My sister! I must help them if I can!*

"So think on this, my children, for it might be the most important thing I can say. Your salvation would be hollow if you don't help each other come home. Remember we are family, and families leave no one behind."

Afterword

Monday, October 4
Chevy Chase, Maryland

The night was quiet, the dark so still and heavy it seemed to suck up the light from the stars. Then the moon disappeared behind a wall of thin clouds, a sudden wind blew, and the night came alive with the sound of fall leaves blowing along the paved lane. The leaves crackled, brittle and dry, a reminder of past summer days. The wind picked up to a howl, almost seeming to moan, blowing a low fog that swept over the ground.

Neil Brighton stared at the dark. He lay restless and agitated; he had been restless all day. He had been restless all week, and he didn't know why. Something was coming—he could feel it deep in his bones—something *moving,* something *watching,* something that was bringing an evil change. He could feel the frustration, but he didn't know what it was. He glanced at his wife, who was asleep on her side, her blonde hair tossed about her, the streetlight on her face. He watched her sleep a long moment, her breathing heavy and slow; then she winced and pulled back, as if she was experiencing the same feelings in her dreams. Neil reached out to touch her, placing his palm on her cheek; she pressed against his fingers and leaned into his touch. But she didn't wake fully and soon was in deep sleep again.

Neil lay back and listened to the leaves rustle in the yard. He felt anxious and tight, a sprinter ready to explode from the blocks. He fought the anxiety, then finally sat up on the side of the bed.

He shook his head to clear it, but the fear only settled deeper in his chest. The blackness seemed to consume him; he'd felt nothing like it before. He glanced at his wife, then pushed himself out of bed.

Something was happening. And it was happening at that very moment.

He walked down the hall, pausing at the top of the stairs. He placed his hands on the rail, feeling the beautifully carved oak. He listened for a moment to the grandfather clock ticking at the foot of the winding stairs, then took a deep breath, fighting the anxiety within. He was surrounded by luxury, the highest house on the side of the hill, but he felt naked and exposed, like standing on the edge of a cliff. He stood a long moment, alone, in the dark.

Then he thought of his sons and turned suddenly for their room, a bedroom they shared at the top of the stairs.

He opened the door just enough to let in a crack of light from the hall. As he pushed the door open, he got a whiff of the smell: sweaty jerseys, leather basketballs, gym bags, a half-eaten bowl of popcorn—the tangy smell of youth that he knew so well.

But his sons were no longer children. They were growing into young men.

They stirred under the blankets, but neither one of them woke. The older son, Ammon Parley, eleven minutes older than his brother, lay asleep on his bed, his hair, blond like his mother's, in a tousle on his head. His younger brother, Luke

Benjamin, dark haired and tan, rolled to his side and turned away from the light. Looking at his children, the father flashed back almost fourteen years, to the first time he held them on the second day of their lives. Eight weeks premature, the two boys were just beginning to prove that they wanted to live. Surrounded by doctors and nurses, machines and tubes he did not understand, Neil had picked up his sons, holding them up one by one, talking to them quietly while staring into their dark eyes. Their bodies were so weightless it was almost like holding a doll, with their tiny heads against his fingers and their feet on his wrist. They were four pounds of perfection, with soft faces and staring eyes.

As he held them, a wave of emotion had swept through his soul. He felt a sense of eternity as the veil brushed his face. In his mind, he saw a vision of who his sons really were, of what they had accomplished on the other side of the veil, of the decisions and choices that had brought them to this time, to this family and place.

"My brothers," he had muttered as the tears rolled off his chin. "My brothers. My children." He swallowed. "My sons."

And now, in the darkness, in the hallway, in the quiet of his home, having been driven from his bed by a dark power that seemed to move across the land, Neil looked at his children and felt much the same way. Staring at their faces, he knew they were greater than he. "My brothers," he muttered as he stood in the hall. "What are your missions? What is the reason you're here?"

He lowered his head as a sudden warmth filled his chest. He trembled and stepped back, a look of awe on his face. He shook his head suddenly and brought his hands to his eyes. He stumbled, his legs so weak he almost fell to his knees.

Heavenly Father had answered his question, at least as

much as he could. He had shown him a vision of what lay ahead.

The last days were unfolding. And Great Ones were here!

"Pray for them," the Spirit told him as he lowered his head. "Pray for your children. Pray for your sons. Pray they will grow into the men that I intend them to be. Pray for the lost one, Samuel Porter, for he was once a great leader who has lost his way. He is alone now and lonely, and I need him on my side. He has no one to turn to, so you must pray for him too!"

Neil shuddered, then pushed himself away from their bedroom and sat on the stairs. All night he knelt in the darkness and prayed as the Spirit had directed him to.

EAST SIDE, CHICAGO

Many miles to the west, the same cold wind blew outside a tenement building, a large and dirty brownstone on the east end of Chicago. A young mother named Mary stared through the kitchen window of her fifth-floor apartment. Six feet in front of her was another brick wall, another tenement building, dirty and blackened from a century of soot. Five floors below her, a homeless man slept on the grate. Steam rose around him, but still he shivered from cold. Mary watched him, then glanced up at the only patch of night sky she could see from her valley of mortar and stone; there were no stars in east Chicago and she could not see the moon.

She reached out to open her dirty kitchen window, pushing up against three or four coats of white paint, but the window held tight. How long had it been since she had opened it? She pressed upward again and the thin pane finally moved. She opened the window a few inches and the cold air blew inside.

She stood by the sink, letting the air chill her bare arms, and took a deep breath to savor the smell. The air had come up from the park, for it carried a faint scent of trees and wet brush. It was quiet outside, at least as quiet as Chicago could be. With the taxies and MLK Highway, the elevated train on its track, music from the bars, and the thugs on the streets, she never heard actual silence, just a reduced roar. She glanced down at the drug dealers on the street corner. They were there every night, come heat, snow, rain, or shine. She wondered when they ever ate, where they slept, where they lived. It seemed they were a permanent part of the sidewalk, like the cracks in the cement.

At forty-three, Mary was small and petite, with silver beads in her dark hair, a thin face and small nose. Her name, Mary Shaye Dupree, was an old southern name that went back three hundred years, back to the mistress of an old French plantation owner on the outskirts of New Orleans. Four generations before, her kin had migrated north, looking for jobs and freedom from the cotton fields.

Mary was a strong and fine-looking women, but her strength was fading fast, for the world and its burdens were bringing defeat. Wrapping her arms around her shoulders, she shivered from the night air. She studied her reflection in the window, staring into her own eyes. Seeing the defeat, she turned quickly away.

Walking down the narrow hallway, Mary came to her bedroom, where her daughter slept on a small mattress on the floor near her bed. Entering the bedroom, she stared at her daughter's gaunt face. She was beautiful still, though her hair had grown thin and her lips were drawn tight. She was sleeping in pain; that was clear from her groans. Mary stared at her daughter and felt the pangs of despair. She was no longer angry; she only felt empty now.

The only good thing she had ever done in her life was taking this orphan and bringing her into her home. The only time she had ever been happy was when she held this child in her arms. For almost six years she had loved her as if she were her own; no, maybe more than six years—she didn't know. All she knew was she loved her until she couldn't love anymore.

And now her little girl was being taken, piece by piece, day by day. The vibrant laugh, the soft hugs, and the wonderful smile—all of it fading, all of it dying away.

Her daughter opened her eyes and looked up at her mother. "I didn't mean to wake you," Mary said quietly.

"I had a very strange dream," Kelly Beth answered, her voice drug out from fatigue.

"Tell me about it." Her mother sat down on the edge of the bed.

"I don't know, Mom. It was so real. So clear. But it doesn't make any sense."

"That's the way of dreams," Mary answered softly.

Kelly Beth waited, catching her breath. "I was watching a funeral," she began. "There was a horse and a wagon, and lots of military men around, and this beautiful little girl—the funeral must have been for her dad. And when it was over, she looked up at the sky as if she was talking to God."

Her mother listened, then nodded. "Is that all?" she asked.

"No, Mom, and this is the part that I don't understand. As I watched this funeral, I had the very clear impression it was for someone I knew, someone close and very dear . . . almost like a brother, I think."

Her mother smiled, then pulled her close. "But you don't have a brother, Kelly."

The girl relaxed against her pillow. "But the feeling was so clear."

Her mother patted her hand, then kissed her cheek. "Think about it," she said. "And maybe you'll figure it out."

The little girl closed her eyes, exhaustion overcoming her. Seconds later, she fell into sleep again.

Mary watched her daughter as she drifted to sleep, then wiped her eyes and slowly lay down on her bed. Lying on her pillow, she stared up at the dark, her mind drifting, unfocused, finding it difficult to concentrate.

She let her thoughts wander, knowing where they would go. She thought of the young men she had seen on the street. Two young men, two young preachers—they looked ridiculously out of place, like baby-faced monks in their white shirts and ties. "Go back to Utah!" her neighbor had mocked as they walked down the street. The boys had smiled and waved to her, then continued on their way. That was two weeks before, and she had not seen them since.

The young mother thought about them, then rolled onto her side. The night passed in silence, but sleep didn't come, for the faces of the strangers seemed to haunt her somehow. Why couldn't she forget them? It made no sense at all. Who were they, these preachers? And why did she burn inside?

Find them! a quiet voice seemed to cry in her soul. *I have a great work for your daughter. Now go out and find them so they can save her life!*

* * *

On that same night, Satan took stock of his kingdom.

The evil hand stretched its cold fingers across the dry autumn land, bringing disappointment and frustration that angered people's souls. Though unseen, it was real, real as the heat of the sun, yet cold as ice water and brittle as bone. To some it brought darkness and a thirst for hate and revenge, jealousy and a lust for power and flesh. To others it brought a simple sense of unease—a sense that something wasn't right, something deep and unknowable, a sense of distress for the future, as if something was coming, a sense of awkward discomfort, as if the world had changed and would never step back. The blackness settled like a blanket, covering the earth like black snow, falling slowly and silently until it draped the whole land.

The evil moved over his kingdom. As he passed, those who held to the light felt a shadow creep over their hearts. Some looked up at the moon, wondering what it could be, while others huddled in the safety only their homes could provide. They took a chill at his coming, hoping the day was not yet. His earthly servants, however, hardly noticed him pass; most denied altogether that he was even alive, and even those who did believe in him were looking for something different, something more obvious, something that fit the common perception of what he would be.

He walked on, always moving, full of dark energy. His work was almost complete and, unlike the old days, he could move freely now, go where he pleased, for he was always invited and most mortals wanted him there. Indeed, his enemies seemed to be falling away. They could hide in their families, they could deny he was there, but that didn't stop him from marching where he would through the land.

And he was growing in power, the great prince of darkness, the prince of this world! The emotion grew inside him, an eruption of pride. He felt cold, dark and arrogant, but justified in conceit.

The shadow almost smiled.

Then a dim beam caught his eye.

He moved closer and snarled as a knot formed in his chest. He moved with more urgency, and the bitter seed grew. The tiny lights grew in number. Then he realized what they were.

These were the Great Ones—the valiant children of God! Looking upon them, he saw the strength of their souls. Another shudder ran through him. So the Great Ones were here. And they were seeking out each other so that they could fight him as one.

As he gazed upon these valiant spirits who had been saved for this day, he realized with a fury that they were not afraid. They knew who they were and what they had done. And because of that knowledge, they had no fear!

He pondered a moment before the memories returned; then a tremble stirred inside him and he snarled again. It was all coming back, memories from the premortal world.

He recognized these warriors; he knew every single one. He knew their names and their faces and the things they had done. He remembered specific acts of courage and their defiance of his commands. Everything he had dreamed of, everything he had desired, had been ripped from his fingers because of what these had done.

So the battle wasn't over. They had come to fight him again.

He sneered with emotion, an unheavenly sound. He had to destroy them. Destroy them while they were young!

The last battle was upon him. But he was ready this time. He had learned many secrets about how to destroy men's souls, and he understood the weakness that was born with the flesh.

He laughed in his anger. He was ready for them. He was more powerful! Let them come with their Great Ones. He was Terrible now.

The Great and the Terrible had assembled.

Let the battle begin.

Sneak Preview

THE GREAT AND TERRIBLE

Volume 2

Even as the Allies celebrated victory,
the appalling costs of the war began to emerge. It had
killed as many as 75 million people around the world.
In Europe, about 38 million people lost their lives, many
of them civilians, a majority of them in their teens and
early twenties. The destruction defies belief . . .
Numbers alone did not tell the story . . .

—PRENTICE-HALL WORLD HISTORY

I say unto you, that great things await you;
Ye hear of wars in foreign lands; but, behold, I say unto
you, they are nigh, even at your doors, and not many years
hence ye shall hear of wars in your own lands.

—DOCTRINE AND COVENANTS 45:62–63

chapter one

OCTOBER 6
KARACHI, PAKISTAN

The Palestinian moved through the crowd easily, for he was comfortable there. Though he was not among his own people, the sounds and scents were the same. He felt the constant press of flesh against him, the movement of the crowd, the chatty voices of women and the guttered growls of men, too busy, too grand to respond to their wives. He smelled the tang of old bodies and felt the gritty dirt on his feet. He felt the uneven pavement beneath him and the glare of the sun, white hot and oppressive, wringing great drops of sweat from under his arms and around the small of his back. Everyone sweated in Karachi; they sweated to keep cool, and they sweated to survive. No one was clean in Karachi. It was just the way it was.

The Palestinian moved around a brown and rusted cement hole in the sidewalk, one of the public toilets that was built without the benefit of even a curtain for privacy. He moved through the crowd, working his way toward a small open-air market half a mile down the street. In the distance, he heard gunfire, a series of quick *pops* and *ratta ta taps* in reply, but he paid no attention. It was almost a full block away, and gunfire in Karachi could be heard every day. In any given twenty-four-hour period, half a dozen citizens lost their lives to petty thieves, gang wars, drug runners, hate, or revenge. The slave trade that flourished on the outskirts of the city was a significant source of the dangerously high murder rate, but it was also a significant contributor to the local economic machine. Teenage captives from China, India, Pakistan, and Afghanistan were harbored in Karachi before being shipped off to brothels throughout the Pacific Rim. Even as he walked, the Palestinian passed a group of three teenage girls bound together. For thirty *dinre* he could have bought any one of them.

Stopping on the corner, the Palestinian waited for a break in the traffic. He glanced quickly around him, turning his back on the street to look in the direction from which he had come. To his side, a roughly mortared brick wall sported an old movie poster. Tom Cruise smiled at him, his long black hair drooping over his eye. The Palestinian frowned and turned quickly away. A break came in the traffic and he moved into the street.

Ten minutes later, he sat down at a wooden table at an outdoor café. The owner moved toward him, then recognized his face and instead turned for the kitchen. Seconds later, he emerged with a mug of hot *cheka* tea in hand.

"Amid," the owner said as he placed the mug on the table. "God be blessed—you are safe. It is good to see you again."

The Palestinian, a tall man with dark eyes and enormous ears, nodded to the restaurateur. "How is your fish?"

"Very fresh, *Sayid*," the café owner lied.

The Palestinian grunted and pointed to his plate. The restaurateur nodded and moved through an open door and into his kitchen.

Minutes later, the Palestinian was eating his meal: char-coaled slab of sea trout, with its head and bones still intact, and a bowl of white rice with hot mustard sauce. The crowd thronged around him, moving up and down the street. An occasional automobile passed by, forcing pedestrians onto the narrow sidewalk and around the small tables of the outdoor café. A group of children played in the street, gleefully chasing each other. A mule pulled a decrepit wagon with one wheel on the sidewalk and the other on the street.

Halfway through the Palestinian's meal, a Pakistani man emerged from the crowd, approached, and sat down without saying a word. In contrast to the Palestinian, who was dressed in a traditional flowing *dakish,* the Pakistani was dressed in black slacks and an open white shirt. Neither of the men was distinguishable in the crowd.

As the Pakistani sat down, Amid looked up and held his fork to his mouth.

The Pakistani lit up a smoke. "Amid Safi Mohammad, how is your meal?" he asked.

Amid Mohammad didn't answer, but pushed in another mouthful of fish. The Pakistani watched him chew, then leaned forward in his chair. Mohammad pulled away as he caught the whiff of cologne. He studied his supplier, then wiped his mouth with the back of his hand. "Brother, I have to disagree with you on this meeting place," he said in a heavy voice. "I don't believe it is wise." The Palestinian paused and glanced to the sky, almost as if he expected to see an American satellite hovering there. Mohammad's eyes darted down the street. "The rats have eyes, eyes like spiders; they can see everything."

The Pakistani nodded. He appreciated his fellow warrior's fear. But they were in his territory now, and he was not concerned. This was his city, his territory. His tribe controlled everything, and he knew every movement of the American spies. His crew had identified every one of them, and they kept a close eye on them. Yes, the Americans got around—that was true—but he also had evidence they were not watching today.

He dramatically crushed out his cigarette. "Mohammad, you have to trust me," he answered knowingly, while nodding almost imperceptibly to the roof of a squat cement building on the other side of the street. "The Great Satan has many eyes, but this is my lair. We are safe here; I assure you. My people are near. That is, of course, unless you allowed yourself to be followed . . . " The Pakistani's voice trailed off. The accusation was clear.

"No, no," Amid Safi Mohammad quickly replied. "I was careful. I followed your instructions to the letter."

"All right, then." The Pakistani sat back and picked at his teeth. "Now, let's get it done."

Amid Mohammad pushed his dirty plate aside. "This will be our last meeting. Our work is almost complete."

"Good. I agree. It has been a dreadfully long year."

"You have done very well, doctor. My people are pleased."

The Pakistani only nodded. If Mohammad only knew! If he had any idea what the Pakistani had gone through. For more than twelve months, he had lived on the edge of a knife, a simple breath away from being discovered. He wanted this over. He wanted it done. It was time to relax, time to enjoy his money. He took a deep breath and forced a thin smile. "The arrangements for the final delivery have been made," he said. "All we have left is to transfer the money."

The Palestinian nodded. "How is your memory?" he asked.

The Pakistani frowned. "Not good, as you know."

"Then get out a pencil and start writing this down."

The Pakistani reached quickly into his back pocket and

pulled out a small pen. He grabbed a napkin as the Palestinian started to speak.

"The payment will be deposited into an account drawn on the Soloman Bank of Malaysia. The account number will be forwarded to you by private messenger later tonight. The withdrawal instructions and authentication codes are thus: authenticate zulu, one, four, whiskey seventy-nine . . . that's seventy-nine, not seven nine, then today's date and my birthday."

The Pakistani scribbled furiously.

"Once you have the account number, the money will remain in the account for only three minutes," the Palestinian continued. "That's three minutes, Dr. Atta, not one second more. If you haven't transferred the money out of the account within the three-minute window, we will take repossession of it. And if that happens, it is over. Our business is done. We will have the hardware, and you won't have anything."

The Pakistani looked up from his writing and frowned. "That will not be necessary," he answered defiantly. "I will make the transfer. Don't you worry about that."

The Palestinian glanced down the street. "I'm not worried, Dr. Atta, but the instructions from my client are clear."

The Pakistani nodded. Amid went on. "Our people at the bank will be monitoring every transfer. Once the money has been deposited into this first account, you will immediately move the money into another account at the same bank. A second messenger will provide you with the specifics pertaining to this account before the transactions begin to take place. Once again, the money will remain there three minutes. Three minutes to make your transfer, or we take possession again. From there, you will move the money into twelve separate accounts established in various banks in the Philippines. After that, you are on your own. We wash our hands of the paper trail."

The Pakistani looked up from his paper. "And the messengers?" he asked.

"Same men as before. You will recognize them both."

The Pakistani sat back and pulled out another cigarette. "Fifty million?" he confirmed.

"As we agreed."

"And the final installment?"

"Upon delivery of the last nuclear warhead." The Palestinian wet his cracked lips.

The Pakistani tightened his fingers around the butt of his brown cigarette. Suddenly, without reason, he began to sweat like a pig. He pressed his lips together and folded the paper napkin into a small square. He studied his client. "So that is it?" he concluded.

The Palestinian nodded. "I believe that it is."

"We will not meet again."

"There is no reason to."

"So tell me, before we separate—I would dearly like to know. Where did you get your money? One hundred million U.S. dollars—that is not a small sum. Who is your financier. I'm dying to know."

"A poor choice of words, Dr. Atta. Be careful what you ask for or you might get your wish."

The Pakistani scowled. "I have provided you with three nuclear warheads—not an easy thing to do. I am taking an enormous risk, more than you could ever know. I control many generals, but I do not control every one. I have put my neck in a noose here, and I deserve to know who is financing this operation."

The Palestinian pushed himself away from the table. "Too many questions, Dr. Atta, is not a good thing. The money will be delivered. That is all you need to know. We want the third warhead by Friday. Now our business is done."

The Palestinian dropped a couple dirty *dinres* on the table and moved into the street.

Two days later, a rusted container ship, an enormous old freighter loaded with barrels of refined kerosene, lubricants, and refurbished electrical generators, left the port at Karachi bound for the Straits of Hormuz. It took only three days to reach the port of Ad Dammam, the huge Saudi port on the eastern shore of the Persian Gulf.

On the burning pavement of the seaside dock, two enormous but nondescript crates were loaded onto the back of a two-ton army truck. The truck pulled away from the warehouse and turned to drive south. Overhead, two helicopters followed its path.

That night, the third nuclear warhead took its place in an underground storage facility on the Saudi air force base of Al Hufuf.

Twenty hours after the last warhead was delivered, Dr. Abu Nidal Atta, deputy director, Pakistan special weapons section, principal advisor on national security to the Pakistani president himself, didn't wake up after his customary afternoon nap. When his wife couldn't rouse him, she immediately called for his personal doctor. He arrived within minutes, but it was already too late. Dr. Atta's heart had ruptured. There was not a thing his doctor could do.

An autopsy was requested by the physician, but the president of Pakistan turned down the request. Following local tradition, the body was cremated before sundown that day.

The Saudi prince in Dhahran smiled when he was informed of the news. He waved his advisor out of his office and immediately picked up the phone. "Get my money back," he commanded. "I want every dime."

THREE WEEKS LATER
DHAHRAN, SAUDI ARABIA

The crown prince of Saudi Arabia sat in the center of his office, an opulent and oval-shaped room with gold-plated walls, muraled ceilings, and diamonds embedded in the molding around the windows and floors. His desk was huge. Three computers and a row of telephones were positioned to his left. A seventy-inch flat-screen TV, the satellite dish tuned to CNN, was built into a wooden console to his right. A wall of huge windows, twenty feet high, looked out on the expanse of desert to the east. The sun beat through the windows, forcing the air conditioner to run overtime and the crown prince to work in his shirt sleeves to stay comfortable.

At forty-six, the prince was strikingly good-looking—tall, athletic, and well-manicured. With European mannerisms (picked up from his five years at Oxford) and a well-cultured voice, he was the epitome of royalty in the modern world.

Though soft-spoken and demurring, the prince was cold and hard and evil to the core. He was a ruthless businessman, a cunning leader, and the great future king. He was the patriarch of his family, and his family was on the rise; he was a great empire builder, just like the sultans before. Living in a world of power, ambition, and pride, he believed in predestiny; and from the time he was young, from the time he could first remember, his mother had told him what lay in store for him. He knew he was chosen. It was as simple as that. His father didn't believe him, nor did all of his kin, but he had proven them wrong, proven it again and again.

There was a soft knock at his office door and, after a respectable pause, the American was escorted into his office. The crown prince stood up from his desk as he approached.

"Drexel, good to see you," the prince extended his hand.

The American walked toward him and shook it weakly. "Abdullah," he greeted, his voice raspy and thin.

The crown prince studied his guest. He is growing tired, the Saudi thought as the old man approached. He looks wrung out and defeated. We need to keep a close eye on him.

While appraising his visitor, the prince kept an easy smile on his face. He pointed to an arrangement of chairs and the two men sat down. Black coffee was ready, which the prince poured for his American guest. The cavernous office was quiet.

"You are ready?" Drexel Danbert asked as he sipped at his coffee.

"Yes, my good friend." The prince sat back and relaxed against his leather chair.

The two men stared at each other. Each played his best poker face.

"You know, I've been thinking," the American said. "Talking around, getting a few opinions, talking in the abstract, of course, but trying to get a feeling for how this will be received. And I have to tell you, Your Majesty, that I believe you are walking on tenuous ground."

"We know we are, Drexel. But you will take care of everything."

The old man was clearly uncomfortable and shook his head hesitatingly. "I don't know, Your Highness. We can do many wonderful things. We've done miracles for you in the past. We are very powerful; our partnerships span the whole of the globe. Yet our friendships are personal, our contacts cultivated and nurtured through both the good and bad years. But there is, after all, only so much we can do, and this plan is far more than we had ever envisioned. Destroy an entire nation! How would you suggest we manipulate the political consequences of that?"

"We won't destroy them. We will move them. There is an enormous difference, my friend."

"But they will not be moved."

"Then that is their choice. If they stay, they will die, but I cannot choose for them. We can't make them be reasonable, though Allah knows we have tried."

"They will not go away. They have nowhere to go. And even if they did, even if they were given other options, they would choose to die in their homeland. It is that important to them."

"Again I will say it: I cannot choose for them."

The American sat back in frustration. It was criminal and inhuman, and though he had sanctioned much human suffering, this was crossing the line. He pressed his lips together; his heart beat in his chest. "How many people will die?" he asked in a low voice.

The crown prince thought and then said, "It is not your concern. This is a conflict between nations, not a criminal case. You are my lawyer, but I am not a citizen of your country. I represent my own interest. I am a sovereign entity. So don't confuse our relationship or overestimate your input here. You are to advise and represent, but don't interfere or give counsel when it is not asked of you."

The American understood and nodded his head.

"All right, then," the prince continued, "if it would make you feel better, I will tell you that it probably won't be as bad as you think. The nuclear weapons are tactical in nature and are relatively small. What we are proposing isn't much different than what has been done before."

The lawyer shook his head. "How can you say that?" he cried.

The prince leaned forward and narrowed his eyes. He spoke with indignation, his voice sharp and on edge. "Dresden," he sneered, "one hundred fifty thousand civilians firebombed. London. Two hundred thousand. Twenty thousand dead in a single attack. Leningrad, three hundred thousand civilians killed in combat, another half million starved. Berlin. Two hundred eighty-nine thousand killed in the last month of the Bolshevik advance alone, and who knows how many in the months before that? Hiroshima. Nagasaki. *Poof!*" The prince brought his fingers together and blew them apart. "A hundred thousand gone. *Poof!* Just like that.

"So get my point, Drexel? This is nothing new. War isn't for the weak. And we've seen this before."

The lawyer frowned and swallowed. The prince's eyes flickered yellow, and Drexel recoiled. Something stirred inside him. Where had he seen that flicker before? He swallowed again, forcing himself to calm down. "Tell me, how many people will die?" he asked as he lowered his eyes.

The prince hunched his shoulders. "Maybe twenty-five thousand in the initial attack. Perhaps another twenty from the radioactive fallout."

The old man stared at his coffee and tried to steady his hands. "And your target is Jerusalem?"

The crown prince sat back and laughed. "Jerusalem? Are you kidding? Do you think I'm stupid, Drexel? Don't you understand me yet?" The crown prince whistled in disgust. Did this man understand *anything*?

The old man stared in confusion. "But if not Jerusalem . . . ?"

The prince waved an impatient hand. "My target is Gaza," he said.

The old man stammered and choked. "Gaza! You're

kidding! That's a Palestinian city! A hundred thousand refugees live in the Gaza Strip."

"I know they do, Drexel. And those who die will die as martyrs. And Allah will receive them unto his own."

Look for the continuation of this story in volume 2 of The Great and Terrible *to be released in the fall of 2004.*